PUFFIN BOOKS

THE
BATTLE OF RIPTIDE

THE
BATTLE OF RIPTIDE

E.J. ALTBACKER

PUFFIN

PUFFIN BOOKS

Published by the Penguin Group
Penguin Books Ltd, 80 Strand, London WC2R 0RL, England
Penguin Group (USA) Inc., 375 Hudson Street, New York, New York 10014, USA
Penguin Group (Canada), 90 Eglinton Avenue East, Suite 700, Toronto, Ontario, Canada M4P 2Y3
(a division of Pearson Penguin Canada Inc.)
Penguin Ireland, 25 St Stephen's Green, Dublin 2, Ireland (a division of Penguin Books Ltd)
Penguin Group (Australia), 250 Camberwell Road, Camberwell, Victoria 3124, Australia
(a division of Pearson Australia Group Pty Ltd)
Penguin Books India Pvt Ltd, 11 Community Centre, Panchsheel Park, New Delhi – 110 017, India
Penguin Group (NZ), 67 Apollo Drive, Rosedale, Auckland 0632, New Zealand
(a division of Pearson New Zealand Ltd)
Penguin Books (South Africa) (Pty) Ltd, 24 Sturdee Avenue, Rosebank,
Johannesburg 2196, South Africa

Penguin Books Ltd, Registered Offices: 80 Strand, London WC2R 0RL, England

puffinbooks.com

First published in USA in Razorbill, an imprint of Penguin Group (USA) Inc., 2011
Published in Great Britain in Puffin Books 2012
001 – 10 9 8 7 6 5 4 3 2 1

Copyright © Razorbill Books, 2011
All rights reserved

The moral right of the author has been asserted

Printed in Great Britain by Clays Ltd, St Ives plc

British Library Cataloguing in Publication Data
A CIP catalogue record for this book is available from the British Library

ISBN: 978-0-141-33997-9

www.greenpenguin.co.uk

MIX
Paper from
responsible sources
FSC™ C018179
www.fsc.org

Penguin Books is committed to a sustainable
future for our business, our readers and our
planet. This book is made from paper certified
by the Forest Stewardship Council.

For Mom and Dad

THE GATHERING STORM

CHAPTER 1

IT FELT LIKE A STORM WAS COMING. THE CURRENT had got colder and faster in the last hour, the way it did in the Big Blue when a squall gathered in the skies above the chop-chop. With all the silt and sand churned from the seabed, it was difficult to see or smell anything from a distance. Gray crept along the side of a massive clump of brain coral and surveyed the area as the others hovered behind him.

"I don't see anything," he said in a low voice, nervously gnashing his dagger teeth.

"I told Snork not to go patrolling by himself," hissed Barkley. The dogfish had been Gray's best friend since he was a pup and had become a trusted voice in Rogue Shiver.

The other members of the Rogue Line present – Striiker, the great white; Mari, the thresher and Shell, the bull shark – waited uncertainly. Everyone was worried

3

about Snork, who had gone missing. It wasn't like the sawfish to leave without telling the rest of the group. No one had seen him for hours.

Fish and other dwellers had cleared the area as the storm neared, leaving it eerily empty. The only sound was the cold water whisking through the forbidding canyons of rock.

"Maybe he just got lost!" Striiker said, a little too loudly.

Mari cut her long thresher tail through the water to quiet him. "Keep your voice down."

"Yeah," Shell added, watching the water above them. "Goblin may not run many patrols through here, but Razor does."

They were in an area off to the side of both the Goblin and Razor Shivers' homewaters. The hunting wasn't especially inviting in these sharp and craggy rock formations, not when there were much better feeding territories in each shiver's own homewaters. Mainly, Goblin and Razor both claimed the territory so the other wouldn't have it.

Since the Tuna Run though, the two warring shivers did share one goal: to *eat* Gray and every member of Rogue Shiver alive. Goblin wanted revenge on them for spoiling his plans against Razor. Fortunately, Goblin didn't have time to search for Gray or anyone else because Razor, the leader of Razor Shiver, was thirsting for Goblin's blood. Razor had barely escaped with his life when he was attacked at the Tuna Run. Now the bull shark leader struck at Goblin Shiver every chance he got. But, given that both Goblin and Razor wanted Gray and the rest of Rogue Shiver dead, swimming here was foolish . . . and awfully dangerous.

"Why would Snork even come here?" Gray muttered to himself.

Barkley fidgeted. "I *may* have said it was a good area to practise stalking."

"You and your big mouth," Striiker said.

The great white and Barkley didn't get along well but pulled together when it was important. Gray didn't want to listen to them argue back and forth for five minutes before agreeing *this* was important. He bumped the dog-fish to stop his snotty reply before it happened.

"Here's what we're going to do," Gray told everyone. He was the leader of Rogue Shiver, so it was up to him to decide the course of action. "Striiker and Mari go to the left side and start searching inwards. Shell and Barkley, you go to the right side and do the same. I'll head to the middle and hunt outwards in a circle pattern."

"What if there's trouble?" demanded Striiker. "What's the plan then?" The great white was first in the Rogue Line, so it was his right to ask. Most of the time, Striiker was a good first: strong and dependable. But he could wear your teeth down with his attitude.

"Signal everyone, then swim and hide. Fight only if you have no other option," Gray answered.

"Let's not waste any more time with dumb questions," Mari said, swimming off to the left.

Striiker grumbled but followed. Mari was Gray's second in Line: smart, capable and level-headed. Barkley gave Gray a nod before leaving with Shell, who was third in Line.

The Five in the Line was an ancient sharkkind invention. Basically, whoever was chosen to lead a shiver of sharks would pick five others to take over if he or she was injured or killed. It was dangerous in the open waters of the Big Blue. Even a fifth could become leader overnight to hundreds of sharkkind in a shiver's general membership. Rogue Shiver was unusual in that there were only six of them in total, Gray as leader and the Five in the Line. They were a bunch of cast-offs and castaways, which was why they had named themselves Rogue Shiver.

Gray caught a descending current into a field of ropy green-greenie so he could swim more or less unseen towards the central area of the maze of rock and coral formations. While the green-greenie would easily hide Barkley, Snork or even a thresher like Mari, the disturbance Gray made ploughing through the field was hardly stealthy. If someone from Razor or Goblin Shiver were looking, Gray knew he would definitely be noticed. Since Tuna Run, he had grown even more, becoming longer and wider than Goblin himself, the former biggest fin around.

"Because you're a freak," whispered a voice inside Gray's head.

He shook his snout, clearing away the negative thought. In a way, Gray was an oddity: the only megalodon swimming the Big Blue in a million years. The members of Rogue Shiver knew he was a meg but still swam with him, flank to flank. Everyone said it made him *special*. Gray chuckled to himself. He used to dream about being the baddest shark in the ocean. Now, when he thought about being *so* different from everyone else, it sent a chill down his spine.

Today Gray would give *anything* to be just another shark in the Big Blue. But he wasn't and never would be.

Gray moved from coral spire to spire. Being in front of a tower of light green coral didn't seem especially smart, so he swam behind a dark blue one. That was more his colour. "Should have been called Blue," he muttered as he began searching the area in the middle of the other two teams.

Nothing stirred except the greenie, bent at an angle by the increasing current. There must be one heck of a storm above, Gray thought.

But otherwise it was quiet. Too quiet.

Gray strained to hear anything out of the ordinary and was rewarded when he detected the muted thrashing of a larger fin nearby. Gray swam in low and fast before gliding to a stop.

It was Snork! The sawfish was trapped underneath a fallen piece of coral, caught by his long serrated nose, which he used to dig for shellheads and other smaller dwellers. "Snork, are you all right?"

"I can't get my bill free!"

"Don't worry," Gray told the frightened sawfish. "I'll have you out in a fin flick!"

"LOOK OUT!" cried Striiker as he hurtled out of nowhere and speared a streaking bull shark in the flank, butting it away from biting Gray.

Razor Shiver!

Barkley took on another bull as Shell rammed a third. It was a melee!

Gray was about to accelerate into an attacking sprint when Shell shouted, "Free Snork! We'll hold them off!"

"Mari, cover my topside!" Gray yelled. The thresher did so, and it was a good thing. She deflected an attack at his dorsal fin with some help from Striiker, who was all flashing teeth and spitting anger.

"Come on, you flippers!" the great white shouted. "Who wants a piece of me?"

Gray got into position to move the large chunk of coral that was pinning Snork. He churned against it with all his might. The coral moved, but not enough for the sawfish to get free. Instead, he yelped in pain.

"Sorry, Snork!"

"It's okay," the sawfish replied, crying a little. "Just get me out of here!"

Gray heard Mari's tail strokes suddenly falter above him. "You've got to hurry!" she told him.

"I am!"

"I mean it!" she urged. "I see twenty more bulls coming!"

Twenty more! Gray and his friends would be torn to pieces!

"Fins up! We've got to move, move, move!" bellowed Striiker as the three attacking bulls were finally scattered. He, too, had seen the other bull sharks coming.

Gray did a lightning quick circle and sped into an attacking sprint. This is going to hurt, he thought, just before ramming the coral that was trapping Snork. Gray could taste his own blood, but the coral snapped into three smaller pieces.

Snork swam off the seabed as Barkley motioned with a fin. "This way!" No one knew the area better than the dogfish, so Gray signalled for everyone to follow.

The group darted into a crack in the ocean floor, probably caused by a seaquake years ago. It was wide enough to swim in, but not by much. Thankfully, it was deep enough to stop the Razor Shiver sharks seeing them for a crucial few seconds.

Everything blurred as they sped through the tight turns inside the crevice, zigging and zagging in silence while putting distance between themselves and the dangerous bulls. After a few minutes, they were in the clear.

"Wow, they don't get much closer than that," commented Shell when they were safely away from the area.

Striiker flicked his fins in annoyance. "We shouldn't

have even been in that situation! Snork, if you do something that chowderheaded again, I'll bite you myself!"

The sawfish dipped his long nose. "I'm sorry. I just wanted to help you spy on Goblin and Razor's patrols."

"It's okay, Snork," Gray said. "But next time, go with Barkley. He's an excellent teacher. And very sneaky."

"I'll help, too," added Mari with a toothy smile. "But let's hope that's the last we see of Goblin or Razor Shivers."

The gang headed into the hidden greenie path leading to the landshark wreck they used as their home and hideout. Gray paused before he joined his friends inside. Night had fallen, and the storm overhead arrived with a vengeance. Gray could feel the vibrations of thunder above the chop-chop. He could see bursts of bright lightning, which caused his skin to tingle each time it struck the water. It was the fiercest type of storm; one they called a flashnboomer.

Gray hoped that Mari was right. He hoped that he and his friends wouldn't see either Goblin or Razor ever again. But Gray couldn't shake the feeling that, like the storm above, the one in their watery world was just getting started.

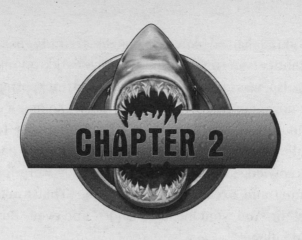

CHAPTER 2

TAKIZA JAELYNN BETTA VAM DELACREST Waveland ka Boom Boom shook his fins from side to side to get some feeling back into them. With his powers, in his youth, he could circle the entire world in a little over a moon, or a month, as the humans called it. But that was many, many years ago. Now, even a fraction of that effort was a chore. Yet when he had received word of what had happened from a quickfin messenger, he knew he must come.

Quickfin was the exclusive news and messaging service for the Big Blue. It was usually reserved for communications and diplomacy between the ancient shivers. Because Takiza shared a long and colourful history with many of these great shivers, he was one of those who received word of the major happenings in the seas.

And make no mistake, the destruction of a royal shiver like AuzyAuzy was a major event.

Takiza had decided to begin training his new apprentice, an interesting young sharkkind named Gray. He was a mere pup, large and inexperienced, only now coming into focus. It would take much effort to mould him into a fin of worth. Sometimes Takiza wondered why he even bothered attempting to pass on his knowledge of shar-kata. Apprentices were forever whining and exclaiming things like, "That's not possible!" or "You want me to do *what*?" and even "But that could kill me!"

So immature.

Using shar-kata, Takiza was able to harness the power in the tides and currents to swim at a rate others might call magical. It wasn't, of course. Mastery of the upper levels of shar-kata bestowed these gifts on the few who could muster the supreme effort and concentration required. Thankfully, Takiza hadn't lost his abilities just yet, despite his age. He swam down the Atlantis and crossed the canal the humans had dug as a short cut to the Sific Ocean. Humans had had a few good ideas – the canal between oceans being one of them. After braving the foul-tasting waters behind a massive ship, Takiza caught a swift current that took him into the South Sific, past the Australia landmass and into Oceania where the AuzyAuzy homewaters were.

Were. But not any more.

The light green-greenie swayed in the slow, warm current as the surviving dwellers drifted in a fearful daze. Unspeakable evil had been done here. From what Takiza could gather, AuzyAuzy had been destroyed by Indi Shiver, another ancient and royal power, originating from the Indi Ocean. King Lochlan I, leader of Auzy-Auzy, now swam the Sparkle Blue, having been killed in the attack. What had possessed these two regal shivers to fight like the brawling gangs that now inhabited the Atlantis? Takiza needed answers.

Not wanting to cause a commotion, he decided to speak with the king's son alone. Slipping by the guards and into the cave was easy for him. "Greetings, Prince Lochlan Boola Naka Fiji," said Takiza.

To his credit the prince – now the new king – did not start, though Takiza had swum up to him unannounced and undetected. This frightened most sharkkind, who thought their senses were fine-tuned.

"Takiza?" The massive great white turned so they could speak face-to-face. Lochlan II projected both grace and power. He was the perfect representation of his kind and the spitting image of his father as a young shark, complete with the telltale golden hue that marked him as AuzyAuzy royalty.

"Your manners are impeccable, young one. But tell me, how are you?"

"Been better." The words hung there. Lochlan's stunning gold skintone sparkled, even in the dim light. The colouring was unique to his great white family and gave the shiver its nickname, the Golden Rush. "You know

Father is dead? The homewaters smashed? Of course, you know. You know everything."

"Not everything," Takiza replied.

Lochlan launched into the story without emotion. "Finnivus came with his floating court. I should have noticed there were too many. We went to hunt off the edge of our homewaters, and they turned on us. Their entire armada was waiting. There were just too many."

Takiza pretended not to notice the tears leaking from Lochlan's eyes. It wasn't his intention to shame the fin. "It is your right to grieve, Lochlan."

"NO!" the golden great white roared. A sleek whitetip reef shark poked her head through the greenie curtain that Takiza had sneaked through, and he yelled, "I'm all right! Privacy, please!"

She darted away and Lochlan went on in a lower voice. "Finnivus and Indi Shiver have to pay! I can get in touch with my feelings later."

"Blood for blood only serves to foul the water," Takiza said. "Your father knew that."

So this was Finnivus's doing. The tiger shark King Finnivus was vain and cruel. That Lochlan had bested him in every contest and hunt the few times they had met when they were pups was a sore point with the Indi tiger. Takiza had hoped Finnivus would grow out of such stupidity and become a good leader. The cold feeling in the pit of his stomach told him this hope was now dead.

Lochlan ground his triangular teeth. "Will you help us? We attack tomorrow."

Takiza winced inside as he saw a sizeable gash on the golden great white's side, probably from the battle. It had been expertly stitched by a doctor and surgeonfish from Lochlan's shiver.

"Absolutely not," Takiza answered with a shake of his gauzy fins. Lochlan stiffened until Takiza added, "But only because you will lose if you act so soon."

"Then we go down fighting. That's the way Father would have –"

Takiza slashed his fins in front of Lochlan's left eye so the great white would be sure to see. "Do not put words in your father's mouth that he would *not* actually say! Your father would want you to protect your shiver-mates, not lead them to their deaths!"

Lochlan quieted and after a moment asked, "What would you have me do?"

"Leave the Sific."

"WHAT?" Lochlan yelled so loudly that the whitetip reef shark poked her head inside once more.

"Is everything –"

"Kendra! Please!" exclaimed Lochlan, and she left quickly. "My first," he told Takiza, which was explanation enough. The new king sighed. "Okay, swim that by me again."

"I would like you to leave this ocean for now. You are the rightful king of the Sific and cannot throw your life away."

Lochlan churned his tail from side to side in agitation. "Do *not* call me that! My father was the king."

"As you wish," Takiza told him.

"I won't swim away from my problems, Takiza. I won't. Finnivus ate my father after the attack. Thank Tyro Mum wasn't alive to see that. You ask too much."

Finnivus *ate* Lochlan I! Takiza's mind reeled. It was something out of the barbarian age. He struggled to hold his own emotions in check. "I am not asking you to swim *away* from your problems. I am asking you to swim *towards* an opportunity. Leave your forces behind and come with a select few."

"Will this opportunity involve a chance to take a fin from that vain and evil fish Finnivus?"

Takiza sighed. "Unfortunately, yes. I believe so."

With that, Lochlan nodded grimly. He swam out of the cave and began giving orders.

CHAPTER 3

"YOUR PRIVATE CAVE IS READY," SAID THE LIONFISH, one of the hosts at Slaggernacks. Even for a lionfish, she was stunning with her vibrant purple-and-blue stripes. But underneath those colourful fins were razor-sharp spines that could inject poison into an unsuspecting victim. "Do you have something for me?" she asked.

Gray was carrying a bonefish he had caught earlier, and now he ejected it from his mouth. This one was barely half a metre long, but bonefish were highly prized and could be seasoned well, which is what they did at Slaggernacks. The place could earn up to six or even eight fish from someone who had a craving for bonefish but was too slow to catch one. That was how Slaggernacks made a profit and kept themselves fed.

"Very nice," said the hostess as she looked over the bonefish. "There's a swell band playing tonight if you're staying around."

"Why don't you show us to our cave?" asked Mari pointedly.

The hostess sniffed but did as requested. After the lionfish had left them at the cave entrance, Mari grumbled, "I really hate this place." She swished her long thresher's tail in annoyance and caught Gray watching. "What?" she asked.

Gray completely lost his current of thought. "Um, other than searching the entire Big Blue, there's no better place to find information about Coral Shiver, and that's why we're here." His mother, Sandy, was the third in Line for Coral, so she would be with the shiver. Or someone from the shiver would know if . . . Gray shook the thought from his mind.

When he had last seen his mother, she was alive and well, and there was no reason to think otherwise. Gray missed her terribly. Frustratingly, neither Barkley nor he had seen a single sign of anyone from Coral Shiver since their epic fight with Goblin Shiver at the Tuna Run.

As if reading his mind, Mari said, "If Goblin, Razor or someone from their shivers sees us . . ." she trailed off, not needing to say anything else.

Their miraculous escape from Goblin and Razor Shivers at the Tuna Run was now the stuff of legend in the North Atlantis. Of course, that would be the case when the mythic Siamese fighting fish Takiza showed up and caused some sort of glowing whirlpool disturbance to suck up Goblin and his shiver, tossing them away like minnows in a strong current.

"That's why we're using the back area of Slagger-nacks," Gray told her. "So we won't be seen."

There were several private caves set apart from the greenie-covered main area. That area was more of a *restaurant* – that was a landshark word – with plenty of areas to hover and eat seasoned fish. When Gray had first tried seasoned fish, he'd hated it, but now he enjoyed it more and more. And there was entertainment from various dweller singing groups. The best ones featured whales and dolphins, although there was a sea horse chorus called *Sea Horsing Around* that Gray liked very much. Gray wondered again how Gafin had thought up the idea for creating Slaggernacks.

Gafin was the king of the sea urchins and used Slag-gernacks as his home base of operations for his tidal pool of murky dealings. It was hard to picture entire shivers of sharkkind listening to a sea urchin, but Gafin con-trolled thousands of poisonous dwellers. The toxic gang included stonefish, octos, lionfish, jellies and many oth-ers, who could send even the biggest fin to the Sparkle Blue. After all, you couldn't be on your guard every sec-ond of every day.

Although no one ever actually saw Gafin, both Razor and Goblin Shivers respected the truce he demanded from anyone who swam in his territory.

This particular back cave had a crisp and cold current

that made it easy to breathe. The secluded greenie-hidden back caves were guarded by poisonous dwellers who protected the safety of those inside and guaranteed their privacy. Supposedly.

"Oww!" Gray muttered under his breath. He had hit his head on the roof of the entrance to the cave. Barkley would have told him his head was getting fatter for sure. Would he ever stop growing? Mari pretended not to notice his embarrassment. Gray liked that about her.

"The dwellers here can't be trusted," Mari said. "What if someone tells Goblin we're here? Or Velenka?"

Gray's mind involuntarily pictured the beautiful and sinister mako shark.

Velenka . . .

She was Goblin's fifth, guiding his fins as if she were swimming for him. She was the one who had told Gray he was a megalodon. She had wanted Gray to rule as a figurehead after getting rid of Goblin and Razor. In fact, Goblin still didn't know that Velenka had planned to betray him right after she had dealt with Razor. Gray was certain he would have been the next to swim the Sparkle Blue after those two.

"Youse wouldn't be meanin' me, would youse?" A random rock in the cave floated off the fine-grained sandy bottom. It wasn't a rock, of course. It was a stonefish named Trank. Mari involuntarily recoiled and moved back. The urge to get away from the poisonous fish was strong in the enclosed cave, even for a shark.

Trank worked for Gafin, but would never point him out. "Gafin likes to keep a low profile," was the greenie-covered fish's standard answer.

"Of course not, Trank," Mari answered. "You're the most trustworthy stonefish I know."

"Well, thanks – hey, wait a second, how many stone-fish do youse know?"

Gray waved a fin at the stonefish. "That's not important."

"It is to me!" huffed Trank. "Us stonefish are very loyal. We stick by our deals, unlike youse sharkkind." The stone-fish gave them a knowing look. Velenka had double-crossed Trank and put him in prison with Barkley, Mari, Shell and Snork. That was how they'd met in the first place.

"Unbelievable!" Mari said, swishing her tail back and forth. "Well, I'm not sticking up for Velenka, so you have me there."

"There you go," Gray told the stonefish. "She admits you're more trustworthy than Velenka."

"That's *not* what I meant," grumbled Mari.

"No take backs!" Trank shouted and whirled his fins to signal the end of this particular current in the con-versation. Mari wanted to continue her argument with the cantankerous fish, but Gray gave her a pleading look and she quieted.

"What have you found out?"

Now Trank seemed embarrassed. Mari leapt into the silence. "Nothing! Again."

The stonefish's small fins circled furiously but then drooped. "You're right. And when you're right, you're right. And you're right."

"Coral Shiver was at the Tuna Run," Gray told the stonefish, his voice rising a little as he slapped the rough wall of the cavern with his tail. "How can no one know anything about an entire shiver?"

"The shiver youse came from was small, and the Big Blue's mighty big – hence the qualifying first part of its name, which is *big*."

"Now's not the time for joking," Mari scolded.

"Who's joking?" Trank replied. "Gafin takes a contract seriously. We're tracking down leads but comin' up empty. I actually think that's a good thing."

"How would that be a good thing?" asked Gray, a bit annoyed. He had been dropping off a steady stream of fish at Slaggernacks for payment and was tired from hunting around the clock to both feed himself and pay the huge number of fish that Gafin demanded in exchange for his help in finding Coral Shiver.

"If we can't find 'em, neither can anyone else," Trank told Gray. "They're smart enough to keep their snouts in the greenie while Razor and Goblin fight it out."

Gray flicked his pectoral fins in frustration. The stonefish did have a point, but it didn't make him feel any better.

Trank chewed on a piece of greenie hanging off his upper lip. He really did look like a sandy stone come to life. "Look, Gafin told me to tell youse he's sorry and youse can ease up on the fish for a while. We'll keep looking, free of charge."

"Really?" Mari asked in wonder.

"Youse don't have to say it that way," Trank replied. "Makes us look bad not being able to find a shiver from the boonie-greenie. Why, just yesterday, I swam thirty kilometres to personally track down a lead I knew was a bunch of chowder, but I went anyway. I mean, whoever heard of a sea dragon named Yappy who never stops talkin' and brags about giant cousins who live down in the Dark Blue?"

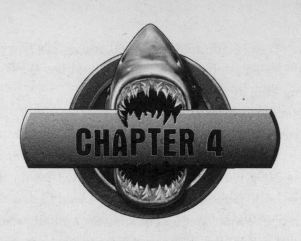

CHAPTER 4

IT WAS A WARM NIGHT WITH GENTLE TIDES AS Gray waited for Barkley to get back. His friend was patrolling again, keeping a sharp eye on both Goblin and Razor Shivers. The exhausted and hungry dogfish finally returned to Rogue's three-level landshark wreck after the moon rose, its glow casting an eerie half-light over the swaying greenie field around the wreck.

Shell, the bull shark, had been nice enough to catch an extra, very fat tunny and save it for Barkley. "This is delicious," the dogfish said between ravenous bites. "I don't know how I missed every fish in the ocean on my way back, but I saw nothing but a couple of wrasse." Wrasse were colourful and smart fish – not like the dumb fish Gray and Barkley had been taught to hunt when they were growing up in the Caribbi Sea. Gray had heard that wrasse weren't very tasty, anyway.

The rest of the Line in Rogue Shiver – Mari, Striiker

and Snork, in addition to Shell – also hovered in the lichen-covered lower level of the ancient sunken ship. "Yeah, you being such a great hunter, it's practically impossible for you *not* to catch a fish whenever you want," Striiker said, bumping Barkley with his pointy great white snout. In the old days there would have been a sting to his words, but now Striiker gave Barkley a good-natured toothy grin.

"Aww, that's not nice," said Snork, waving his long serrated bill with a frown.

"I was only kidding," Striiker explained. "Did everyone get that I was kidding?"

"I got it, I got it," said Barkley. "Good one. I know I'm not the best hunter, but this was different. Never seen anything like it. It was like something had chased every fish in the Atlantis away." The dogfish turned to Striiker with a grin. "But we know that since you weren't there, the fish didn't run away from your ugly krillface, so it must have been something else!" Barkley gave the great white a confident tail slap.

Gray marvelled at the change in his friend since they first swam into the Big Blue as scared pups. Barkley had followed him out of loyalty and friendship after Gray had been banished from Coral Shiver. They'd gone through some tough times. At one point, they were so angry with each other they didn't speak at all. But even when they were fighting, Barkley could always be counted on.

One of the small things Gray appreciated was that Barkley had insisted on being fifth in his Line. After their victory over Goblin at the Tuna Run, Rogue Shiver had made Gray their leader. He'd appointed Striiker as his first but wanted Barkley to be second. "A tiny dogfish as your second?" Barkley had said sarcastically. "Are you out of your jelly-brained mind? Do you want to get Rogue Shiver laughed out of the Big Blue?"

Gray grinned at the memory as he tapped his tail against the side of the landshark boat, making an impatient thumping noise. Mari shook her head. "Why don't you just tell him?"

"He's eating," Gray said. "Don't want to interrupt."

"Tell me what?" asked the dogfish, his mouth full.

"Trank gave me some interesting information –"

"Awww, Gray. Not the stonefish again." Barkley gnashed his teeth as if he had tasted a bitter mackerel. He didn't like anyone from Slaggernacks, but especially not Trank.

"Wait, listen," Gray told him. "Trank said he'd heard of a sea dragon who tells wild stories about his huge cousins in the Dark Blue."

"Yappy!" exclaimed Barkley.

"Do *you* think there might be more than one Yappy?" Gray asked.

Barkley shook his head. "No way. Who would have thought his non-stop talking would actually work in our favour?" He flicked his fins up and down in excitement. "So, go on. Where are they? Is everyone okay?"

"Well, that was kind of it," Gray replied.

"What do you mean, 'kind of it'?" asked Shell. "Didn't that muck-sucking stonefish actually *find* this sea dragon for you?"

Striiker joined in. "I would have thought that with all the fish you've been bringing to Slaggernacks, they might actually do some work." The great white churned his tail so hard it caused loose greenie to fly everywhere. He didn't like Trank much, either.

"Trank did try and find him," Mari told everyone. She swished her shapely thresher tail in a figure of eight, signalling everyone to calm themselves. "But Yappy wasn't there. Neither was anyone else from Coral Shiver."

"So they've moved on," Striiker said, nodding to himself. "Smart."

"Could be," Gray answered the great white. "Or maybe not!" He flexed his tail, full of nervous energy.

Barkley looked at him. "Why are you so happy?"

"Because Coral Shiver was always good at hiding."

"You think they're still around?" Barkley got a little more excited when Gray smiled. "You think they're still around! Somewhere between here and our old reef! Of course! Close enough so it feels like home, but far enough away to get lost!"

"So?" asked Shell. "So what? Does anyone else get this?"

"The thing you don't understand is that *nothing* can stop Yappy from talking," Gray said as Barkley nodded in agreement. "If they were just moving from place to place like drifters, we would've picked up their trail."

"How do you know they didn't just leave the area entirely?" Shell asked. The big bull shark rubbed his rough hide on one of the broken beams of the land-shark ship, clouding the water with a mist of tiny wood particles.

Striiker sneezed and glared. "How many times have I told you not to do that?"

"But my flank itches!"

Gray slapped the great white with his tail, stopping the argument before it began. "Coral Shiver wouldn't have gone off to the Sific or somewhere on the other side of the Big Blue."

"How do you know that?" asked Striiker. "We were ready to go to the Sific to hide from Goblin."

Mari swirled her long tail as she did when thinking intently. "But we didn't. Once sharks find a place that feels like homewaters, we do like to stay there."

"That's true!" said Snork. "I don't want to leave here because I like it!"

"Look, I know you think you're good at sneaking around –" Striiker began, but Barkley cut him off.

"I *am* good at sneaking around," the dogfish said. "But I know what you're worried about. We'd have to skirt the edge of Goblin's patrols and go through part of

Razor Shiver's territory. But it's not like I haven't done it before, you know, that's what I did tonight."

"But you weren't leading Gray," Shell commented. This did quiet Barkley as it was true. It was also the main reason why Gray didn't go searching for his mother and Coral Shiver in the open waters with his friend. Gray was too large not to be noticed on a long swim. But this time he wouldn't stay behind.

"I'm not sticking my snout in the sand and turning turtle while you swim into danger," Gray said, smacking his tail against the hull of the landshark boat with a BOOM! "I'm coming with you and that's that."

Barkley gave Gray a little snout bump and asked, "So when do we leave, big fin?"

The answer turned out to be immediately. Gray wanted to wait while Barkley got some rest, but the dogfish wouldn't hear of it. The journey from the North Atlantis to the edge of the Caribbi Sea took nearly two days. Not because it was that far, but because Barkley insisted that he lead the way and swam so *slooowly* it was unbelievable. He knew the patrol routes of Goblin Shiver by heart. That was the easy part. It was after that, when they got to Razor Shiver territory, where things really slowed down. The dogfish took Gray through thick green-greenie and tight lava canyons whenever he could.

"Sharkkind hate swimming through areas like this," Barkley whispered while heading into yet another field of thick-beyond-belief blue-greenie.

"Add me to the list because I hate it, too," Gray answered quietly. It was awful. This type of greenie felt like it would catch in his gills or wrap around his tail and send him to the Sparkle Blue. There were stories of haunted greenie that would reach out and snare you if you weren't careful. If a shark couldn't swim, he couldn't breathe. This wasn't that type of greenie, though. It was, however, a kind that tickled Gray's snout unmercifully.

The dogfish seemed to have no trouble whatsoever moving through it, which made Gray simultaneously proud of his friend and annoyed with himself. But he was four times Barkley's size, and that probably had something to do with his lack of stealth.

"Move a little slower," Barkley suggested. "You're . . . causing the greenie to sway, umm, more noticeably than when the tide moves it naturally."

"Just say I'm fat," Gray told him, whispering a little louder.

"Hey, I didn't –"

"I can tell you're thinking it!" Gray shot back.

Barkley motioned at him with a fin. "Maybe you're *supposed* to be fat!"

Gray was caught by surprise. Could that be true? Was he supposed to be fat? Barkley knew he was a mega-lodon, though neither talked about it for fear of someone, even a dweller, overhearing. He shook his head at Barkley. "Nope. I'm just big cartilaged. And you'd better not share your theory about my fatness with Striiker or anyone else from Rogue, or I'll –"

"*Shhh*!" Barkley hissed, making a chopping motion with his fin.

Gray immediately quieted and strained to listen. He heard the tide moving the greenie all around him, a few shellbacks scuttling in the sand below and smaller fish swimming by. Nothing large was in the immediate vicinity of Gray's sharp senses. And thankfully, there weren't the telltale chopping tail strokes of a bull from Razor Shiver speeding up to attack.

But further away . . . there was something. Gray could smell the drifting scent of a group of sharkkind. It was too distant to identify what type of sharks, but there was a large gathering somewhere. Gray's nose tingled as he focused on the scents in the water: fear, anger and excitement. It was like a growing storm. Barkley sensed the same and began picking a path leading away from whatever was going on. Gray stopped him. "Maybe it's Coral Shiver."

"Much more likely it's Razor Shiver." That was true. They were near Razor's homewaters. If there were more than ten sharks in one place, they would probably be shiver sharks.

"Barkley, we have to see. For my mum – and your cousins. We have to be sure they're not in danger."

The dogfish nodded and led them slowly through the greenie and towards a low rock formation where they would be able to see upwards while remaining hidden themselves. Gray followed, letting Barkley find the way. The dogfish really was very good at stalking around unseen.

Gray copied the way Barkley moved, alternately shimmying or drifting depending on the current. He found that by doing this he caused less disturbance in the greenie and moved more silently. He was about to compliment Barkley when suddenly the dogfish's tail jerked as if he'd been shocked by an eel. "Back, back, back," his friend whispered urgently.

Gray lowered himself on to the seabed, trying to become a part of it. "What did you see?"

"Razor Shiver."

"How many?" asked Gray.

"All of them, I think."

Gray's heart thudded in his chest as he looked upwards, the sun shining dimly into the ocean from its place high above the chop-chop. There they were! Razor Shiver! He could see their outlines clearly. At least a hundred bull sharks. More, even! They were arranged in loose rows, hovering at the ready.

"What are they doing?" Barkley whispered.

"That's a battle formation," Gray told him quietly. "But the better question is, 'Who are those sharks they're about to fight?'" Gray pointed a fin across the waters to more than four hundred sharkkind lined up against Razor Shiver.

"*Whoa*," Barkley breathed in a raspy whisper.

CHAPTER 5

PLEASE DON'T LET MY MUM AND CORAL SHIVER be a part of this! Gray thought as his stomach heaved. The sharkkind facing Razor Shiver weren't just a shiver – they were a *battle* shiver! Goblin had told Gray those didn't even exist any more. The strange mariners had markings on their flanks that didn't look natural. They were tattoos! That meant these sharkkind were Indi Shiver!

What were they doing so far from their home-waters? Here they were, perfectly ordered and facing off against Razor Shiver. They hovered motionlessly in the strong current as Razor and his shiver sharks struggled to maintain their own formation. Thankfully, Gray saw no one from Coral Shiver. His concentration was so complete he didn't hear Barkley until his friend brushed against him.

"Sink and hide!" the dogfish whispered urgently. It

was then that Gray noticed *another* group of sharkkind. These were in no hurry at all and glided on the lazy current. This wasn't a battle formation as these hundred or so sharks were definitely not ready for a fight.

They were here to *watch*.

Gray took a moment to figure out that these sharks were a royal court, like the ones he'd heard stories about in Miss Lamprey's class at school. While the sharks in the Indi battle shiver all had the same tattoo – a series of never-ending black waves running down each flank – these sharkkind's markings were different and much more intricate.

The young tiger shark leader was the most decorated of all. His tattoos were thin lines forming whirls and swirls, like stormy ocean waters. These covered the white of his belly and the underside of his fins along with most of his flanks. Gray thought the marks looked kind of ugly, even though they were colourful. The sleek tiger shark had a wild look in his eyes and lounged on top of a blue whale, which acted as a kind of mobile throne. Gray looked around and saw there were actually multiple whales, each with a Speakers Rock somehow pressed into its back. When one whale needed to swim to the surface to breathe, another smoothly slipped in, so the royal fish didn't have to flick a fin. Usually a Speakers Rock would be located in a shiver's homewaters, so this was odd. Did Indi Shiver think they had a right to all the water in the Big Blue?

The current flowed just so, and Gray could hear the tiger shark leader perfectly as he giggled a high-pitched titter. "I'll bet my new herald gets eaten! Anyone want to wager the seasoned head of their first in the Line he gets eaten?" Gray's stomach involuntarily clenched in horror. Was the wild-eyed leader joking?

"What do you think, Tydal?" the royal asked, showing off the tattooed underside of his fins.

A brightly coloured brown-and-yellow epaulette shark answered. "King Finnivus, this lowly court shark would never presume to know!"

So the leader was a king and his name was Finnivus. Gray wasn't impressed. He would have been far more interested to meet Tydal, the epaulette shark, because his bright brown-and-yellow markings were fascinating.

"Watch this! Watch what happens!" yelled King Finnivus, his tail swishing with a weird, stuttering excitement. The herald was saying something to Razor. After a moment, Razor's eyes widened in surprise, then anger. He roared and took the herald's dorsal fin with one clean bite.

Finnivus cackled from the back of the blue whale. "Looks like I'm going to need a new herald! Again!"

"Yes, Your Magnificence!" answered Tydal, the court shark. "I'll see to it at once!"

"Mariner Prime, have my armada attack!" Finnivus told a battle-scarred tiger shark, who was hovering by an odd device containing lanternfish. The lanternfish inside were kept perfectly still by a metallic grate holding them gently in place. If Gray had had to guess, this device was something made by landsharks. The lanternfish flashed a series of coloured patterns. Once they had finished flashing, the entire armada attacked. Gray marvelled. Indi Shiver was using the lanternfish as a signalling device!

There was loud yelling by the bulls of Razor Shiver. Gray recognized this for what it was: fear. The attackers didn't waste valuable energy yelling, and this made their silent, whooshing charge all the more terrifying. Next to the discipline of Indi's battle shiver, Razor's mariners were about as dangerous as a drove of tuna. And their fate would be similar.

The attackers charged towards the already disorganized resistance. Gray could see that most of the younger sharks in Razor Shiver weren't holding their place in formation – some even bolted the opposite way, swimming into their shivermates and causing confusion.

Gray looked over at Indi Shiver's commander, who was signalling to the armada with the lanternfish device. His five-layer formation broke off into three columns that twisted and turned like sea snakes. The first column was made of heavy sharkkind to batter the enemy: great whites, tigers and, of course, hammerheads. They swam in snout to snout, mauling the defenders.

The second battle fin was organized for endurance; threshers and bull sharks would feint an attack, but then draw back. Being the best swimmers, they wouldn't tire easily. When they did attack, it was usually from behind as they possessed the strength to swim around the entire battle waters and still make a concentrated strike. The third battle fin included the fastest sharkkind: blues, spinners and makos. When they joined the battle, they widened the cracks in Razor Shiver's defensive formation caused by the other two battle fins.

After only a few fin flicks, there was blood everywhere. Razor Shiver's formation was compacted into a tight ball, useless for either defence or offence. It was a slaughter. Then two Indi Shiver sharks – a blue shark and a mako – struck at Razor himself, one mauling his dorsal, the other taking his right fin.

Razor was finished!

Gray couldn't believe it. All this time, Goblin could never beat Razor, and now Razor was swimming the Sparkle Blue just like that! His large shiver, one that Gray and all of Rogue Shiver constantly feared being discovered by, had been destroyed in less time than it took to eat a bluefin tuna!

The armada ceased its attack and circled what was left of the terrified Razor Shiver. "Whalem, destroy them to the last!" King Finnivus yelled.

"My king, their leader is dead," the mariner prime said. "These remaining bulls could become valuable additions to your armada with proper training."

"They are a disorganized mess!" Finnivus screeched. "Kill them all!"

"King Finnivus, your father would offer mercy."

For a moment, it seemed as if even the noise of the injured and terrified bulls from Razor Shiver subsided. The sharks in the royal court held their breath. Apparently, questioning the cruel king's orders was not done.

Finnivus smiled, showing his notched and pointed tiger shark teeth. "Of course, you're right!" he exclaimed. "My father put you in charge of the armada those many years ago because of your experience, so I should listen to what you think!"

The commander was wise enough to say nothing as Finnivus went on with his mocking praise. "Who am I to disagree with your considerable age, Whalem? Mercy for those who stop fighting, but any who flee must die! Now, forward! I need my rest. Conquering the Big Blue is very tiring!"

And so King Finnivus and his court swam into the heart of Razor Shiver territory and made themselves at home.

CHAPTER 6

A LITTLE BLOOD IN THE WATER WOULD NORMALLY sharpen a shark's appetite.

Not today, though.

Gray wanted to throw up. He gaped at the carnage, never having seen anything like it. Torn bull sharks from Razor Shiver littered the ocean floor. A few dying, finless torsos even crashed into the greenie field he and Barkley were hiding in. These sharks didn't need to be mauled further and were allowed to drift from the fight. Their piteous wails were unnerving but there was nothing to be done. If you lost a fin, the only place you'd swim was the Sparkle Blue.

Gray was cold inside. He waggled his fins just to feel himself move. Nothing he'd learned from Goblin about battle shivers and fighting in formation covered what had just happened. Had Indi Shiver found Coral Shiver and done *this* to it already? Was his mother ... gone?

"Razor's dead," Barkley whispered in wonder. "Do you think any of his Line is alive?" The remaining bull mariners, less than half, were divided into small groups. They would become Indi Shiver sharks or else. Join or die.

"I vote we don't stick around to find out," Gray told his friend.

Barkley nodded and began picking his way through the greenie. They were some distance from the battle waters when Gray felt a prickle run down his spine and recognized it for what it was – danger!

"Swim!" he shouted to Barkley. The dogfish made a crazy turn just as a mako crashed into the seabed where he had been an instant before, getting a mouthful of sand for his trouble.

Gray managed to shift to his left before a blue shark struck in an equally vicious manner. The slight move was enough to cause the attacking shark to miss his dorsal. But only just!

Gray couldn't believe that these two sharks, not much bigger than Barkley, would come after a shark his size. But whatever they lacked in size, these mariners more than made up for in speed and cunning. The two swam in tandem, weaving and switching position like greenie in a strong tide. They turned and came again.

"What do we do? What do we do?" cried Barkley, hysteria creeping into his voice.

Gray gave him a tail slap to the flank. "Get above me and stay there!" Luckily Barkley was good at close-order swimming. Gray could feel the dogfish right above his dorsal. When Gray had become leader of Rogue, he'd ramped up the training a few notches. Striiker loved it, but the rest of the shiver had grumbled. Despite all his considerable complaining, Barkley had learned a few things since Tuna Run.

"Make sure they don't peel you away!" Gray reminded.

"Right!" Barkley answered in a hiccupping voice, switching his tail back and forth to gather speed. "I've got it." The dogfish needed to protect Gray's topside from attack if they were going to survive.

"You can swim, but you can't hide!" yelled the mako as the pair came forward in a rush. The two sharkkind performed an attack Gray recognized as Hake Sideslip, with both doing the move in its mirror opposite as they constantly swapped positions. It was incredible. If he survived the next minute, Gray would have to rethink all the moves he'd learned from Goblin.

The Hake Sideslip faked a snout-to-snout ram, but then rolled into a sideways attack on a back fin. Since the two sharks were doing the move together, Gray couldn't counter with Waving Greenie as he had been taught. If Gray did that, one of the two attackers would have an easy strike on Gray's left or right pectoral fin as both couldn't be defended at the same time.

Instead, Gray did a rolling turn and angled away in a very common move called Grouper Swims Away. Usually shortened to Swim Away, this was basically the same as fleeing. The important thing was to not swim in terror. You needed to keep looking for a way to turn the situation to your advantage and go back on the offensive.

"So even though you're swimming from a fight, you're swimming away with *purpose*!" Goblin had told him, before saying that he himself would never, ever, use such a cowardly move. Here, though, there was no choice. Gray wasn't experienced enough to match himself against the two well-trained mariners and protect Barkley. He needed to use his size and strength to his advantage. But how?

Gray slipped into a falling current of colder water and plunged downwards into a thick kelp bed. He felt the green-greenie scrape past his flanks. Strands even got caught in his mouth, but he ploughed forward anyway. The Indi mariners closed the distance. They weren't afraid of a little seaweed, either, and this was what Gray was counting on. He hoped Barkley would understand what he was doing. Yelling directions would defeat the purpose.

Gray found a coral pillar that was big enough. He

accelerated, whipping his tail back and forth, then cut a turn completely around the coral. The move was called Sea Snake Protects Its Tail. Some of the combat moves Gray had been taught were named in confusing ways, but this one was easy. Every shark made the mistake of trying to catch a sea snake by the tail when they were young. What that got you was a bite on the snout!

When Gray emerged from behind the pillar of coral, he was zooming straight at his two attackers. Surprise! Gray smashed into the mako, snout to snout. He weighed much, much more than the shark and heard its spine audibly snap. It sank, a surprised look frozen on its face.

The blue shark was taken by surprise and lost its forward speed. Before it could do anything, Barkley bit it in the gills – a small bite, but lethal. The blue shark keeled over and sank, warm blood rising from the wound.

"Oh, no," Barkley said. "What did I do?" Then the dogfish threw up.

Gray heard other patrols in the area and didn't know what his next move should be. They had beaten their attackers with a combination of luck and skill. If they met another pair of Indi mariners, their luck would end for sure. Most likely they would pay with their lives.

"Keep down!" hissed an urgent voice. "Get low, or you'll be seen!"

Gray turned to the voice and couldn't believe his

eyes. "Onyx!" he whispered. The blacktip was a member of Coral Shiver's Line.

"Is he really here?" Barkley asked in a dulled voice. "Or are we dead?"

"We're not dead," replied Onyx. "But we will be if you don't stay quiet!"

REUNIONS

CHAPTER 7

"SWIM LOW AND SLOW," ONYX TOLD THEM. "Don't churn up any sand, or they'll see us. You think you two can do that?"

Gray was flabbergasted! Even though he and Barkley were searching for *anyone* from Coral Shiver, it was still a shock to see Onyx. Was Gray's mother nearby, too? Was she all right? There were so many questions to ask, but they couldn't stop and talk. They were in serious danger.

"We can do it," Gray said, pushing the shocked Barkley forward. "Nice and easy."

"Always were a load of trouble," Onyx muttered under his breath. The blacktip led them through algae-covered canyons of rock. Luckily there was plenty of waving greenie floating up from the bottom to hide their movements, as Barkley wasn't swimming at his sneaky best. Gray risked taking a peek at the sun-mottled water above and breathed a sigh of relief when he saw no sharkkind.

After another four hundred metres, they came to a sheltered area surrounded by colourful coral. Gray's heart thudded louder and louder as Onyx guided them through a hidden swimming lane. It blocked the view from above and to the sides – just like the one leading into Coral Shiver's old homewaters.

The swimming wound this way and that. It would be easy to lose your way, and that was the point. Gray's mind raced as the path finally opened into a large central area.

"Where are we? What is this place?" Barkley whispered. He was still stunned from the fight.

Gray's heart leapt when he saw Prime Minister Shocks, the old moray eel who had been the leader of the Coral Shiver dwellers since Gray was a pup. Morrison, the crusty old crab, was busy arguing with Timmons, the sea snail! Aqualina, the red tang, was speaking with Dundee, the sunfish! And there were others, too! Shocks saw Gray, and the eel stopped the conversation he was having with Kanter, the sea horse leader. Soon everyone was staring. It got so still and quiet, Gray heard the water whisking past the algae-covered rocks around them.

"Hi, everyone," Gray said in a soft voice.

The silence remained deafening. Gray was about to say something else when he saw her. There, hovering off to the side by a blue coral spire covered with lumos, was his mother. She had been hidden earlier by the same pillar of coral. Now she stared at him as if she couldn't believe her eyes.

"Gray?" she asked, her voice catching in her throat.

Her mouth and nose barbels vibrated so much, he could feel the movement in the still water. It tickled a little, like when he was a pup.

"Mum!" He swam to his mother, bumping her a little harder than he meant to. She skidded sideways and scattered a colourful group of tangs. "Mum, Mum, Mum!" he yelled. "You're here! You're actually here! I – I missed you so much!"

"*Shhh*, it's okay, Gray," Sandy told him, rubbing his back with her tail.

Gray felt tears well up in his eyes. "I can't believe it's you! I can't believe I finally found you!"

Onyx swam up to them both. "So, I picked up this wayward shark for you to question."

Sandy chuckled, crying freely. "Thank you, Onyx."

"Like a bad clamshell, this one," the blacktip said with a grin. "I guess we can't get rid of him. And maybe that's not so bad." Onyx looked Gray over from snout to tail tip. "He's grown. Again. And learned how to fight."

Sandy grew concerned. "What do you mean?" she asked. Gray's mum looked at him crossly, her barbels now pulsing as they did when she was mad. "What happened?"

"I – we – didn't want to...." Shame reddened Gray's

face and his tail drooped. He had just sent another shark to the Sparkle Blue. It would have been unimaginable when he was a pup.

"They had no choice, Sandy," Onyx told her. "I was watching the Indi patrol and saw them dive and attack. I figured it was Razor Shiver survivors – Razor's gone, by the way – and then I saw these two." Onyx flipped his tail in frustration and spoke to Gray. "I would have helped, but you were too far away. Where did you learn that move? Both of you fought well."

Gray looked over his shoulder at Barkley. Some of the dogfish's colour seemed to have returned, but he was still shaky, listing to the side a little.

"I – I feel sick again," Barkley muttered.

Onyx tapped the dogfish's flank with his tail to steady him. "It was him or you, Barkley. Did you want it to be you?"

"We wouldn't want that!"

Barkley turned and saw his cousins. They were all there! Barkley started crying his eyes out as his family enveloped him. Seeing his friend flank to flank with his loved ones got Gray welling up again. Pretty soon he gave himself over to laughing and crying and rubbing against his mum. But he didn't care. It felt so good!

He even met his new brother and sister, Riprap and Ebbie. They were little nurse shark pups who couldn't speak yet and mostly hid in the greenie, but they smiled at Gray. Both had the cutest little barbels of their own, just like their mother. He immediately loved them. What an overwhelming joy that his family was safe and sound!

They talked for hours, catching up. Gray and Barkley didn't get all the details of the attack by Razor Shiver that had destroyed Coral Shiver's reef, but they didn't really want them. Even now, it was obvious that most of the sharks and dwellers here were still dealing with the currents from that terrible day.

It turned out that no one in Coral Shiver knew the attack was really the work of Goblin and Velenka. Quickeyes, who had been first but was now leader of Coral Shiver because of Atlas's death in the attack, wanted every bit of information. After the story, he looked to Sandy (who was now second in the Line) and Onyx (first) and said in a low voice, "One day, maybe we'll get a chance to talk with those two."

Everyone in the circle knew that there would be no conversation involved. Gray hoped Quickeyes wouldn't go looking for trouble. Even though the thresher was a strong shark, fighting Goblin wasn't a smart thing.

Gray and Barkley recounted all their adventures. Sandy puffed with pride when Barkley told them Gray was the leader of Rogue Shiver. She gave her tail a swirl and smiled as she had when he'd got a good grade in class. For his part, Gray was totally embarrassed. He blurted out, "It's a really small shiver, though!"

After a while, he noticed that everyone was listening

– really listening. Quickeyes and Onyx were asking for Gray and Barkley's opinions, weighing their words as if they were real shiver sharks. There was actual respect in their eyes when Barkley told everyone about stopping Goblin's plan to take over the North Atlantis at the Tuna Run.

After Barkley was finished, Gray asked, "Why choose this place? Why settle so close to Razor Shiver?"

"It wasn't planned," Sandy answered. "We swam away as fast as we could, and this was where we stopped to rest. It's hidden and can be defended, two things that were very important right then."

"Yes," agreed Quickeyes. "It was the best we could hope for under the circumstances."

"Goblin once told me about sharks with markings called tattoos. They were named Indi Shiver, from the Indi Ocean. The sharkkind that fought Razor Shiver had those. Could it be them? The Indi Ocean is so far away."

"Yup," Onyx said. "They're Indi Shiver."

"How can you be so sure?" asked Barkley.

"Because," Onyx told them, as he turned and showed his own tattoos, "I used to be a member."

CHAPTER 8

EVERYONE SETTLED INTO THE MAIN AREA OF the new Coral Shiver homewaters to listen. There the spires of rock and coral were covered by yellow and green moss, trailing long strips of greenie as the current moved through the shelter. Onyx had quite a tale to tell. His own shiver had been conquered by Indi when he was just a pup, but it hadn't been bloody.

"Their king at the time was Finnivus's father, Romulus," Onyx told everyone. "He was a good and wise king who took in our wandering shiver, which was searching for better feeding grounds."

King Romulus let them become part of Indi, and Onyx was put to work as a hunter when he was barely older than Gray was now. Later, Onyx became an Indi mariner and swam with the armada, which was nicknamed the Black Wave. "That's how I got my tattoos," the blacktip said. He showed the markings that Gray and Barkley had long ago thought were just odd but natural – and totally gilly. But now that Gray had seen the black wave pattern up close, as well as in battle, he didn't think they were cool at all.

"So you know them?" asked Gray. "You know Finnivus?"

"I saw him many times while he was growing up. He's a couple of years older than you. Since he was the prince, I tried not to go anywhere near him. He was a spoiled brat."

"Obviously, he's got worse," Sandy remarked.

This was an understatement, of course. "One day, I was hunting with King Romulus and the royal court, including Finnivus. We both went after the same fish. I was young and jelly-brained. I should have let the prince have the strike, but I beat him to it. Finnivus got mad and ordered my death."

"What kind of shiver is this?" Gray asked incredulously. "It was a *fish*!"

"They have their own rules, and I dishonoured the prince," Onyx replied. "Their laws may be harsh to us, but according to them I was wrong."

"But you're still around," Barkley said, pointing with his fin. He seemed to be doing better since their escape earlier in the day. "What happened?"

"King Romulus would never disgrace his son by taking my side in front of the royal court. He told a commander to carry out the prince's order. Maybe Romulus knew he wouldn't do it, maybe not. But the commander swam me out of sight and let me go. He said to never come back. So you see, Gray, you're not the only one who's been banished."

"Tell them about the commander," said Quickeyes.

"Ah, here's where it gets interesting. That commander's name was Whalem."

"That's the name of the shark Finnivus called the mariner prime," Gray said thoughtfully.

Onyx nodded and swished his tail. "Exactly. They are one and the same."

"You're sure?" Barkley asked. "Are you positive?"

Onyx nodded. "You don't forget the shark who spared your life."

"Do you think you could talk with him? Make the mariner prime get Finnivus to change his ways?" asked Barkley.

Onyx shook his snout back and forth. "Whalem would never disobey his king."

Barkley whipped his tail through the water. "He spared your life, didn't he? Isn't that disobeying?"

"Or was he obeying a king who secretly told him to let me go? I don't know."

"You were a member of the armada," Gray said. "Do you know how they fight? What their weaknesses are?"

"Sure, I know their formations, but that's not enough. Their mariners are well-trained, and in the hands of a good mariner prime, which Whalem is, they are unbeatable."

The group spoke for another hour, before everyone drifted apart. Gray and his mother went off alone. The day had brought one huge surprise after another. Gray wondered if he could bear one more, but knew he must take up the subject. He pointed at Riprap and Ebbie, still hiding in the greenie. They were intensely interested in their giant big brother but too shy to swim up close.

"Riprap and Ebbie are so cute," he told his mum. "Aren't they?"

"Much cuter than I am," Gray said evenly. He didn't want to upset his mother, but he had to continue. "They have barbels, just like you, and fan-shaped teeth, just like you. I don't have those...."

His mother's barbels twitched in a way that Gray had never seen. He didn't know if she was angry or hurt or thinking. Then she finally said, "I've been waiting for this day. In some ways, I hoped it would never come."

Gray forced himself to be patient while his mother gathered her thoughts. It was obviously hard for her.

"The truth is I found you, alone and scared in the ocean far, far away."

The words passed momentarily without Gray realizing what they meant. But then he did. "So...you're not my mother?"

Sandy rubbed his belly with her tail. "Of course I am, Gray. I raised you and fed you and loved you. I'll always love you. I'm just not your birth mother." Tears leaked from the corners of her eyes and were carried away by the tide.

It felt like the Big Blue was spinning round and round, and Gray was tumbling tail over snout.

"I know this is hard, but I love you. You can tell me anything, Gray. Even if you're mad at me, it's okay."

"I'm not mad, Mum. I just have so many questions," he hiccupped.

"I know," she soothed. "I'll answer what I can."

"Did you know I'm a megalodon?"

Sandy's mouth hung open in surprise. Her barbels moved left and right as she shook her head in wonder. "I didn't. But I knew you were special."

Special. There it was again. Only this time it just added to the storm of confused feelings Gray was having. He was beginning to hate being *special*. "Where do I come from?"

"The place I found you was almost in the Dark Blue. It was deep and ancient. The very mountains shifted, and there was a huge volcanic eruption. It became so bright, it was like a red sun had fallen into the ocean. I almost died. And there, in the dark, with the water tasting of sulphur – I found you. That's why I named you Gray. The entire Big Blue seemed grey that day."

He couldn't help it and laughed. "You named me Gray because the water was mucky and stank?"

His mum gave him a little tail slap to the flank. "That is not the reason." She grew quiet before continuing. "It seemed like the ocean itself *changed* so it could have you swimming in it. It was incredible and terrifying. But most of all, it was a day unlike any I've lived in my life. I knew right then it was my job to take care of you."

Gray hugged Sandy with his tail for a long time. But then he asked his last question. "So my parents could be alive?" Gray wasn't sure which answer he wanted to hear.

Sandy shook her head. "I'm sorry, but I don't think so. If there was another megalodon in the ocean looking for you, I would have heard about it. And I stayed in the area for a long time to make sure. I think your parents died saving you. You see, they must have also known you were special." This time the word didn't feel so bad.

Gray asked his mother not to tell anyone that he was a megalodon, and she agreed that keeping the secret was a wise thing for now. That was a mystery for another day. Right now, Finnivus was threatening everyone Gray cared about. That problem demanded all his attention.

But there was one more thing. . . .

"Can I still call you Mum?"

"Of course, you can!" Sandy said, her eyes leaking tears. "Always and forever, Gray."

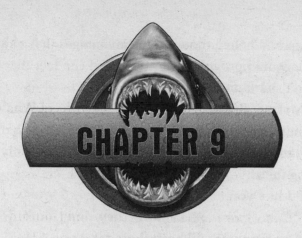

CHAPTER 9

WHALEM WATCHED AS THE RAZOR SHIVER prisoners were herded from their homewaters, each bull between two armada sharkkind for the long swim to the Indi Ocean. There they would be broken down before being raised up into Indi Shiver mariners. Right now, the prisoners' fins drooped and they swam listlessly, having been easily taken apart in battle. Of course they had lost. This *shiver* was no more than a gang of thugs. And to allow only one type of sharkkind to be members? That was foolish.

Whalem had once tried to get Finnivus's father King Romulus to allow dwellers into the Indi armada as equals. That was the one time had been a total disagreement between them. Romulus thought that only sharkkind should be allowed into his glorious armada. Dwellers could serve in different ways, as the blue whales or lanternfish did, but could not be Indi armada mariners. Whalem thought the advantages that a swarm of eels would provide far outweighed the fact that they weren't sharkkind.

"Mariner Prime, you called?" asked one of Whalem's commanders, a bull shark. A commander led each of the four battle fins of the armada, but this was the only bull among them.

"I'd like you to talk to the prisoners," Whalem told him. "Calm them. Make sure they don't do anything stupid or Finnivus will have them for lunch."

"He might, anyway."

Whalem let his commanders speak on equal terms when they weren't in official settings. He believed the sharks who fought flank to flank with him deserved this measure of respect. But it wasn't the time for this sort of talk in the ranks. "What do you mean by that, commander?"

"I – I . . ."

"Surely you aren't suggesting that the king would dishonour Indi Shiver by harming surrendered prisoners?"

The bull cast his eyes downwards, dipping both head and tail. "No, Mariner Prime! I misspoke."

"Plainly, you're tired from the battle."

"Yes, Mariner Prime!"

"I don't want you saying any such thing to the other commanders, is that clear?" Whalem said, making his eyes like volcanic rock. He could not afford to let rot like this begin. Once started, it was impossible to stop.

"Yes, Mariner Prime!" the commander answered, dipping his head once more.

"Now, see to the bulls," Whalem told him. "I'm sending you because you are a bull yourself. So it's up to you. Will you help me save their lives by making sure they join Indi Shiver happily and without reservation?"

"Yes, Mariner Prime!" he exclaimed. "I live to serve you! I mean – I live to serve the king! It seems I am very tired, Mariner Prime, forgive me."

"On your way, then." Whalem shook his head after the commander had left. Some in the armada probably did have more loyalty to him personally than to Finnivus, even though it had been five years now since Romulus swam to the Sparkle Blue. But Whalem would not use that loyalty, as some had asked him to. He could no more betray Romulus's wishes now than when they'd been young. And Romulus had always wanted his son to be king. "Now if only Finnivus would believe that," he muttered silently into the current. Whalem had thought the young king was going to have him seasoned and served for lunch for disagreeing with him earlier. That the young pup would even think about bloodying the waters further after their crushing victory made Whalem's stomach turn. And this was also after the disgrace they had committed against AuzyAuzy Shiver!

AuzyAuzy was the only shiver that could have given the Indi armada a tough time. Finnivus had never liked

Prince Lochlan, or his father. He was jealous of Auzy-Auzy Shiver and its reputation in the Big Blue as the most honoured shiver. And golden-hued Prince Lochlan was loved and respected by everyone. While the body of his father, King Lochlan, had been found, the prince's had not. So many sharkkind had been killed in the frenzy during and after the battle that Finnivus was sure the golden great white was swimming the Sparkle Blue. That was the reason behind Finnivus's attack – he hated Prince Lochlan. Well, that and the fact that Finnivus was a power-hungry fish who wanted every sharkkind and dweller in the ocean to bow before him. Whalem felt his stomach turn. Such dishonour! Such disgrace! He would never feel clean again after witnessing the horrors Finnivus had wreaked upon AuzyAuzy.

Finnivus had none of his father's mercy, grace or intelligence. Indi Shiver needed replacements for its mariners who had died, were injured, or grew too old to fight. Killing a group of disorganized and terrified enemy sharks when a battle's outcome had been decided was a strategic blunder that showed bad leadership. The best way to turn a beaten shiver into loyal Indi mariners wasn't to terrify them with cruelty.

If only the battle had ended just a bit earlier, thought Whalem. Every fin flick the king delayed had put more blood in the water, which every Razor Shiver shark would remember. Swimming to the royal court, Whalem sighed. Such a waste.

Finnivus watched as the decorator crabs and fish wove Indi Shiver symbols into the greenie which grew in the area. "Pfah!" the king grumbled. "What a low and lowly place this is! Isn't that right, Tydal?"

"No place in all the Big Blue is as glorious as your own Indi homewaters, Magnificence," answered the brown-and-yellow court fish. "But we do try."

"Try harder," was the king's bored reply.

"Immediately, Your Highness!"

Finnivus gave a non-committal grunt. Whalem suppressed a smile as he thought of Tydal's nickname among some of the armada: First Court Toady. The epaulette shark was required to see to every tiny detail that tradition dictated. He did his work well.

Whalem nodded at the king's Line, all friends of Finnivus. Their parents were Indi royalty, as evidenced by their intricate tattoos. The young sharks had been secretly against Finnivus taking his rightful place on the throne, but now hovered under his belly like remora. Five years ago, these supposed friends had thought that Whalem should take the throne when Romulus died.

Whalem knew this wasn't because of their tremendous respect for him as their first in the Line. No, it was because he was more than seventy summers old and had no children. If he became king, one of them would rule within a few years. Thankfully, the others of Romulus's old Line sided with Whalem and voted to make Finnivus king. They weren't here any more, though. Whalem was the last of the old guard, kept in position because he remained undefeated in battle, and Finnivus was a superstitious fin.

"Three cheers for King Finnivus!" yelled the second in the Line, a tiger.

"Finnivus Victor once again victorious!" the third cried immediately afterwards.

Whalem especially disliked it when they did that: one yelling something, followed by another emphasizing the point in a different way. They were being sucker fish! But Finnivus didn't seem to notice. The king flicked his pectorals, preening. "Oh, please! I – I mean, *we* – only do what *we* are meant to!"

Finnivus *loved* the royal *we*, but didn't always use it correctly.

Whalem sighed as his eyes slid to the now nearly invisible Tydal. The brightly coloured court shark could hover perfectly still and seemed to disappear through sheer motionlessness. Probably a good trait for a court fish to have when Finnivus got angry, Whalem thought.

Finnivus slapped his tail enthusiastically against the Speakers Rock as the seasoned head of Razor Shiver's leader was brought to him on the back of a sea turtle. Whalem used the tide to drift further away from the meal. It turned his stomach. Though Indi Shiver had a tradition of eating an enemy shiver's leader, Romulus had never, ever honoured it. But Finnivus had brought back the ritual. Whalem shuddered as Finnivus ate with gusto.

"Oh, this is delicious! I can't wait to see who I'll get to eat next!"

A prickle of fear marched down Whalem's spine. Had he made the wrong choice when he had refused to be king of Indi Shiver? One poor decision, one tail stroke out of place, and it could be his head on that dining platter. Whalem shivered.

CHAPTER 10

"GRAY, THIS IS ABSOLUTELY THE WORST IDEA you've *ever* come up with," Barkley said as they waited in a thick kelp bed outside Slaggernacks. It had taken most of the day to carefully creep through the greenie from Coral Shiver's hiding place and skirt Goblin's territory to get safely into the neutral area around Slaggernacks.

"Quiet," Gray whispered.

"I didn't think you could top your other classics," the dogfish went on. "You know, like when you got banished from Coral Shiver? Or when you decided joining Goblin Shiver was a good idea? Or when you listened to Velenka instead of me? How about when you –"

"*Shhh!*" Gray said as he bumped Barkley in the side. "Quit being such a tail bender, will you? We have to do this."

"Why? Why do we have to?"

Gray looked at Barkley. "Because it's the right thing. And you know it."

"Doesn't mean I have to like it," the dogfish grumbled.

"Could you at least be more quiet in your dislike?" Barkley made a face that Gray pretended not to notice. "There they are." Sure enough, Goblin and Velenka were swimming into the back cave at Slaggernacks. "Don't forget the fish," Gray told Barkley as he left the greenie.

The dogfish shook his head and muttered, "This is so dumb," before grabbing the huge sea bass. Barkley was right. This wasn't smart. But it was a calculated risk that Gray hoped would work out.

Barkley dumped the plump bass by the door. Trank gave him a nod and led them inside as a large octopus dragged the tasty fish away.

The dogfish shook his head and waggled his fins nervously. "Such a bad idea."

When they got to the cave where Goblin and Velenka were, the reaction was immediate. "WHAT ARE THEY DOING HERE?" shouted the furious great white. He gnashed his teeth so hard that one cracked off.

Velenka was just as agitated when she saw Trank. She had double-crossed and imprisoned the stonefish.

"Relax, Velenka. This isn't what youse think. And youse, too, Goblin," Trank said.

Goblin glared balefully at Gray. "Didn't I teach you

anything?" he seethed. "At least challenge me to a snout-to-snout fight."

"Some other time," Gray told them. "Razor's dead."

"What?"

"Are you hard of hearing?" Barkley asked sarcastically.

"One day I'll eat you, doggie!"

"Like you wouldn't for no reason at all," the dogfish replied, churning the water with his tail. "Suck algae, you big bully."

Trank swam between them, little fins turning dainty circles as dust and debris fell from his upper body. "No one is doing anything to anyone in Slaggernacks unless Gafin says so! Youse get me?"

Goblin leered at the small fish. "Think you can slow me down if I wanted to do something?"

Trank motioned upwards with a fin. "Not me, personally. But it just so happens it's not just me, personally, who's here."

Everyone looked up. Hundreds of urchins and poisonous dwellers, including blue-ringed octopi and stingrays, hung on the ceiling of the cave. If Goblin attacked, there was no way he'd get out of the cave without being stung many, many times.

The tension in the room vibrated in Gray's lateral line and spine, but the great white didn't charge. He motioned to Velenka and she broke the silence. "How do you know Razor's dead?"

"I saw it," Gray told the mako, her blacker-than-black eyes boring into him. "Half his shiver went to the Sparkle Blue. The rest were taken."

"Taken by whom? Why should I believe anything you say?" snorted Goblin. "What kind of game are you playing?"

Barkley shook his head. "You should have just let them drift right into that whirlpool."

"They call themselves Indi Shiver," Gray persisted.

Goblin snickered. "Indi's homewaters are halfway around the Big Blue!"

"They fight in coordinated formations and would take your mariners apart in a fin flick," Barkley said. "Turns out your little playtime practice drills are good for nothing!"

Gray slapped the dogfish with his tail. "Barkley! You're not helping." He turned to Goblin. "But he's right. Even at our best – with ten times our numbers – the fight would be over in minutes."

"What do you mean by *our* best?" the great white sneered, showing his teeth again.

"What *do* you mean by that?" asked Barkley.

Gray smiled at both of them, a little embarrassed. "I, umm, didn't mean that, I guess." He looked at Goblin and Velenka. "But I know what your shiver can and can't do. And what Indi Shiver did to Razor and his bulls was nothing short of . . . horrifying."

Goblin chuckled. It started as a slow rumble but

then grew and grew. "Only a turtle like you would say that Razor being eaten was *horrifying*."

Velenka gave Goblin a calculating look. When she saw Gray watching, it vanished. "Maybe we should listen to the meat of the message. Razor and his bulls were smashed by some shiver."

"Right. By *Indi Shiver*."

"Whoever they might be," Velenka told him.

"Why are you really here, pup?" Goblin snapped his jaws, the serrated edges of his triangular teeth scraping together. "You want to make nice so I forgive you?"

Barkley shook his head and muttered, "Such a bad idea."

"I'm here because you did teach me a few things, and for that I'm grateful," Gray said to the barrel-shaped great white. "I'm here because your shiver sharks aren't evil and don't need to die. But lastly, I'm here because I think no one, not even you, deserves what happened to Razor and his shiver."

Goblin's gills pumped in and out, hate making his eyes glow in the darkness of the cavern. While Gray hadn't been expecting the great white to get all weepy and say everything between them was okay, this wasn't the reaction he'd envisioned.

"I told you once, pup, our homewaters are worth fighting for. If you don't understand that, I never taught you anything. Come on, Velenka." Goblin swam past

Gray brusquely, his crescent-shaped tail slapping Barkley in the face on the way out. The dogfish took it in silence.

When Velenka left, Gray asked her, "Will you talk with him?"

"I'll try," the mako replied. "It's good to see you."

"Feel free to keep moving, sister," Barkley told her.

"How do you know we won't wait for you outside?" she said to Barkley with menace in her voice, her pitch-black eyes boring into him.

Barkley just smiled. "Because I made a deal with Gafin and your friend Trank. If I go missing, you'll get a visit when you least expect it. So you'd better hope I stay healthy."

Velenka glanced warily at Trank, who was speaking with some other stonefish on the far side of the cave.

"Did you really do that?" Gray asked Barkley after the mako had gone.

"Of course not!"

Trank swam over to them. "If I'd known the meeting was gonna be *that* tense, I woulda charged youse more."

Gray and Barkley swam out of Slaggernacks soon afterwards. They scooted into the cover of the greenie and made their way to the landshark wreck. "That didn't exactly work out," Barkley commented.

"I did what I had to," Gray told him.

"So, what's next?"

"I think it's time to make the introductions between Rogue and Coral."

"Finally." Barkley gave Gray a stinging tail slap to his belly. "An idea I can really get behind." The dogfish tore through the greenie as fast as he could.

Gray gave chase, the tension of the meeting melting in the crisp current. "Oh, you'd better swim!"

CHAPTER 11

BECAUSE GRAY HAD BEEN THERE BEFORE, HE was able to lead his friends to Coral Shiver's new homewaters even though the entrance was well-hidden. The trick was to approach from the east and look for the rock formation shaped like an upside-down lobster tail someone had named Rock Lobster. Once they got there, a shiver shark Gray didn't know led them into the hidden swimming lane and through the long fronds of green-greenie. Barkley and the other Rogue members followed in single file until the path widened into the secluded reef. The shiver shark told them to wait there until Quickeyes was informed of their arrival.

Shell tapped Striiker with his flipper. "Hey, do I look okay?"

"What do you mean?" the great white asked, genuinely confused. "You look like you always do."

"You're sure? Do I have a mackerel head in my teeth or anything?"

Striiker sighed and didn't answer, flicking his tail instead.

"You've been edgy all day," Barkley told Shell. "Don't worry. These fish are family."

"But my ex-family attacked your family," Shell replied, his tail switching right and left. That was true. Goblin had used sharkkind from Razor Shiver to do his dirty work.

"We've been through this," Gray said. He knew his mother wouldn't blame Shell for Razor Shiver's actions, but to be safe he'd sent word before their visit that they would be coming with an ex-Razor Shiver bull shark. He couldn't be absolutely sure how everyone else would react, and he didn't want any surprises. "It wasn't your fault, Shell."

Quickeyes and Onyx swam over with Gray's mother. There were introductions all round, and then Rogue Shiver toured the reef. It had interesting coral formations that shone with ghostly yellow and blue hues. The sea moss covering the rocks underneath was light green and fluffy as it waved back and forth in the current. It wasn't their old reef in the Caribbi Sea, but it was nice.

They heard Yappy before seeing him. The little sea dragon came tearing through the greenie where he'd been hunting, shouting, "It's Gray and Barkley! It's Barkley and Gray!"

"Not again," muttered Onyx to Quickeyes at exactly the same time Barkley said it to Gray. This made everyone chuckle as the little dweller zipped between Gray and Barkley.

"I knew it was you two when I heard your voices, on the account of it *is* actually you two!" Yappy exclaimed. "Have you guys seen the coral on the other side? It's pretty gilly, all right! Pretty *and* gilly, I mean! How do you think coral got its name? I mean, what if we called it *gracklenut*? I suppose coral sounds better than gracklenut, though."

Snork, the sawfish, chimed in. "Gracklenut sounds more like that rough kind of orange-greenie. Maybe we could start calling *that* gracklenut!"

"That's a great idea!" said Yappy, his attention now thankfully focused on Snork. "Who are you? Have you named many other things?"

"My name's Snork," he answered. "I've always wanted to name things, but never got round to it."

"You definitely should find the time. I can tell you'd be good at it. Why, I'll bet we could go around the reef, and you would name three or four things right now. Do you want to?"

"That sounds like fun," Snork replied. The pair swam off, to the amusement of everyone else.

"So that's Yappy," Mari remarked.

"Yep," Gray said, nodding.

Barkley motioned with his tail at the retreating

figures. "That's a dangerous combination." When everyone laughed, he added, "I'm serious. Those two? They might never stop talking. Ever."

"Snork seems like a good fin," Quickeyes told Gray. "Like the rest of your new friends." After that, the discussion grew more serious. Onyx took Shell off to the side, and they spoke intently by themselves, probably about Shell's history with Razor Shiver. When they returned, the blacktip seemed at ease with the big bull shark.

For some reason, Gray's mum and Mari were talking. A lot. After every other sentence, they glanced Gray's way and chuckled.

A horrible thought hit him. The bucket story! What if his mum told Mari the bucket story? When Gray had been a young pup, he'd explored a galleon – a different kind of landshark ship from the one Rogue Shiver lived in now – and had got his head stuck in a bucket. It was wedged on so tightly that Prime Minister Shocks had had to get help from the octopus clan to pull it off. Everyone had called Gray *buckethead* for a long time after that. His mother and Mari laughed again, but louder. "Not the bucket story, Mum," Gray muttered to himself.

"So, what do you think?" Quickeyes asked Gray. "Will you and Barkley join our Line? You'll be third, he'll be fourth."

Gray was dumbfounded. He just clicked his teeth,

not knowing how to answer. Barkley came tearing over and gave Gray a fin bump. He had obviously been told.

The news travelled fast, and pretty soon everyone, even Snork and Yappy, were back. The colourful sea dragon was actually silent for once.

"Are you surprised?" Sandy asked Gray.

"Definitely, Mum. Definitely." Gray wanted to accept Quickeyes's offer, but something nagged at him.

It was Striiker who brought what was troubling him into focus. "I'm happy for you," the large great white began, "but right now, with everything that's going on, you can't be a member of two Lines! Your loyalty has to be to just one."

"Your friend is right," said Quickeyes. "I wish he wasn't. But it's your choice."

"Rogue will respect whatever decision you make," Mari added.

Sandy swirled her tail to get everyone's attention and announced, "Either way, Coral and Rogue should be allies. If any of you are in trouble, you can always come here."

"Are you serious?" Shell asked. "Really?"

Onyx gave the bull shark a slap on his flank. "Any friend of Gray and Barkley's is a friend of ours."

"Well?" asked Barkley.

Gray wanted to say yes. He really did. But Goblin was still out there. If Gray joined Coral Shiver, the evil shark might attack his family again. Gray wouldn't take that chance. But before he could tell everyone someone else spoke.

"He cannot!" said an oddly accented voice. "He promised himself to me."

Everyone started as Takiza seemingly appeared from nowhere and settled into the centre of the council discussion. It was a moment before anyone could speak.

"And who are you, exactly?" Quickeyes asked.

The tiny fighting fish ruffled his fins with a flourish. "I am, exactly, Takiza Jaelynn Betta vam Delacrest Waveland ka Boom Boom."

"Huh. I pictured him bigger," Onyx mused. Takiza featured prominently in the story of how Rogue Shiver had stopped Goblin and Velenka's plan at the Tuna Run. When Gray had told the story, he could see that the members of Coral Shiver didn't totally believe him. Now their disbelief was replaced by amazement.

Quickeyes swam up to Takiza. "You're really him? The same Takiza who Gray said saved a family of turtles? The Takiza who saved a whale calf from fifty makos when my father's father was a pup? The same Takiza who stopped a tidal wave from washing away an entire reef between the AuzyAuzy and Zeeland land masses? You're *that* Takiza?"

The little betta bobbed his head and snapped his filmy fins straight out for a moment. "The same."

"Why do you want my son?" Sandy asked, her nose and chin barbels vibrating.

"He is my apprentice. He must come with me for training."

"Training for what?" Mari prodded.

"Why, to defeat Finnivus Victor," Takiza said matter-of-factly. "After Finnivus declares himself emperor, of course."

VELENKA
STRIKES

CHAPTER 12

VELENKA TRIED TO CONVINCE GOBLIN THREE times that they couldn't hope to survive an Indi Shiver assault fighting snout to snout. A scouting party had confirmed that the armada was camped at Razor Shiver's old homewaters. Of course they were. Ever since the Tuna Run, it seemed as if Goblin Shiver had been caught in a whirlpool of misfortune. First, their plan to get rid of Razor had been blocked by Gray and Rogue Shiver. After the Tuna Run, Razor Shiver had launched a series of successful attacks against them. And now that Razor and his bulls were gone, a new and much more powerful force – the Indi armada led by King Finnivus – had taken their place and threatened to annihilate Goblin Shiver. Indi continued to send out large patrols from their new homewaters, but they were content to stay close to that area. For now.

"Ha!" Goblin had snorted. "They're scared to come out!"

Velenka knew why Indi Shiver wasn't interested in probing their defences. Indi could crush them any time. When Goblin had ordered an ill-advised ambush, the outnumbered Indi patrol didn't even pursue after absolutely mauling Goblin's forces. The tattooed mariners hadn't been surprised for more than an instant. Their defensive formations and lightning-quick counterattacks easily won the battle. Ten Goblin Shiver sharkkind had been killed, with just six getting back to safety.

If only Goblin hadn't made it back, Velenka thought. But he had and insisted on getting ready for the *father of all battles*, as he called it. The situation was hopeless.

"Where are we going?" Goblin asked.

"Hydenseek," she answered. Hydenseek was an area inside Goblin Shiver territory just off their homewaters where big fish hunted the small fish that gathered in and around a thick field of blue and green-greenie.

"Pfaf!" he snorted. "If I wanted seaweed, I'd order it at Slaggernacks. Let's hunt the open waters."

"You go if you want." Velenka gave him a smile and a friendly swish of her tail. Encouraging him to go was taking a gamble, but she didn't want to reveal that she had an agenda, so she acted nonchalant. If Goblin left right now, Velenka would have to come up with a different plan. As it was, she'd waited two nerve-jangling days for everything to click into place.

Indi might come for them tomorrow, so she had to act today!

Thankfully, the great white flicked his crescent tail in annoyance but followed. Velenka led him into Hydenseek where the greenie grew denser and denser.

"So, you might as well start," Goblin said.

"Start what?" Velenka asked.

"Talking me out of what I'm planning," Goblin grumbled.

The last time she'd tried to do that, Velenka had thought the angry great white would send her to the Sparkle Blue. "I'm done with that," she said. "Swim your current. I know I won't change your mind."

"Finally!" He laughed. "I've worn you down." He snapped up a fat mackerel that was too slow in recognizing the danger Goblin represented.

Velenka wasn't going to end up like that mackerel. "Something like that," she told him as she angled in a slightly different direction.

"Where are you going?" he asked. "The greenie's too thick there."

"I think this way is going to be lucky for me," she replied. "But if you're scared, I'll meet you later."

The great white followed, of course. He was so predictable.

It was only a few tail strokes later that she heard Goblin grunt in pain. Velenka turned and saw he didn't realize what was happening. Finally, the great white recognized the blue-ringed octo hanging on to his tail, bending it back on to itself.

"Can you believe this?" he said. "The little flipper is attacking me! *Me!*"

Velenka remained silent as the octo hung on to Goblin's tail, injecting him with its poisons.

"Krillfaced coward!" Goblin shouted. He slammed his tail against the nearest rock. One octo, even a blue-ringed octo, wasn't enough to kill most full-grown sharks. Certainly not one as big as Goblin. No, it would take more than that.

So Velenka had arranged for more.

A dozen stonefish floated up from their hiding places in the moss-covered rocks below where they had been waiting for days. The toxic dwellers stung Goblin on his belly and by the bends of his fins.

Goblin screamed in frustration as the stonefish kept low and underneath him. He mashed a few with his serrated, triangular teeth. He received a huge sting in the gums when he scored one bite. "Oww!" he yelped. "This is why I never come here!"

Velenka realized she should have been saying encouraging things. Or acted scared for him. Velenka was doing neither – because she was the one behind the attack.

And with one look into her black eyes, Goblin knew it, too.

"Traitor!" he shouted. The great white darted

forward, but she was quicker, avoiding his lunge. The poison was working. And with the octo entangling his tail, bending the top half downwards, Goblin couldn't swim at full speed. But his rage provided a momentary edge. He almost caught Velenka with a quick rolling turn, but she dived underneath a coral lattice, and he got a mouthful of rock for his efforts.

"I'll ki-ki-kill you," he slurred. The poison was working. But she hadn't left anything to chance.

The delicate box jellyfish floated eerily through the water towards Goblin. How it moved, she didn't really know. This cube-shaped jelly was the most toxic predator in all the Big Blue. Goblin stiffened as if he had swum into an invisible wall when the jellyfish stung him in the gills. The stonefish below his belly struck at will – Goblin's futile snaps no longer worried them.

The box jelly continued stinging, now floating over Goblin, attached to him by more than twenty translucent tendrils. It was a terrible sight, but Velenka couldn't look away. She had never heard of jellies dealing with sharkkind or dwellers, even in ancient times. That Gafin could offer their services was remarkable. She would have to be careful in dealing with the urchin king.

With a last audible hiss, Goblin rolled belly up. The great white was paralysed and dying but stared hatefully as Velenka glided towards him.

"I tried to tell you," she said. "But you wouldn't listen. Do you think everyone is so eager to die for your *honour*? No, we're not."

Then Velenka bit Goblin in the gills.

As she swam away, small fish and crabs gathered to eat.

CHAPTER 13

IT HAD BEEN THREE DAYS SINCE THE SPIRITED discussion with Takiza at the Coral Shiver homewaters. The ancient betta had insisted that Gray should come with him right that minute. He wasn't big on explaining anything to Striiker, whom he called "a shark with chowder for brains", or even to Quickeyes, the Coral leader.

But Takiza *did* answer questions from Gray's mother. Through her, the little betta had managed to convince everyone that it was a good idea for him and Gray to swim off together. Gray believed it was a good idea, too. He had been so excited to train with the mysterious and powerful Takiza – fish of legend! What an honour! Gray thought he would travel with his new teacher for a few days, all the while learning cool, mysterious secrets!

That was then. Now, he was miserable.

"Again!" Takiza bellowed. Gray followed the lightning quick Siamese fighting fish through a forest of razor sharp coral spires. "Faster!" The spires, while colourful, were hidden by curtains of greenie growing from the ocean floor. Takiza was training Gray in waters much deeper than those he usually swam. They were in an area two days east of Goblin Shiver territory, almost smack in the middle of the North Atlantis Ocean. If they continued a few more days, they would reach the lower edge of the Atlantis Spine, the huge mountain range that formed the guiding landmark of the Tuna Run. If they went a few days further than that, they would be hovering where the tuna actually swam.

The Big Blue was very deep here, almost at the point where it became known as the Dark Blue. But even at this depth, which Takiza said definitely wasn't the Dark Blue, it was uncomfortable and gave Gray the shivers. He wasn't sure whether that was from the colder temperature, the eerie darkness, or the water that physically pressed against him. Gray hadn't believed that the water was *actually* squeezing him until Takiza explained that the weight of all the water above them caused that feeling.

And yet this depth was nothing, apparently. Gray could see the ledge underneath his right flank fall away into total blackness. Takiza told him that this giant hole in the ocean floor was called the Maw. It did kind of look like a huge mouth that would eat you if you were foolish enough to swim there. Inside the Maw was where the Dark Blue actually began. Supposedly, only prehistore nightmares lived in the Dark Blue.

Gray hoped Takiza wasn't going to make him go any lower – especially into the Maw. The blackness terrified him. As it was, the sun was only a pale afterthought, a wan light far above the chop-chop that he felt more than actually saw.

Gray heard a muffled crack as he was shoved by the fierce current into a coral spire, snapping it in two. He winced as Takiza glided over.

"No, no, no!" Takiza yelled in a surprisingly strong voice. "Why must you swim like a pregnant sea cow? You are sharkkind, so swim like sharkkind!"

Gray could barely speak at this depth because of the strain against his throat. Mostly, he just took the abuse in silence. But there were times, such as now, when he got frustrated. Gray wanted to shout, roar even, but the best he could do was whine in a high voice. "I'm trying!" he squeaked. The pressure also made him light-headed and loopy, which was one of the reasons he kept running into things.

"Make your way *around* the coral – not through it!" Takiza scolded. "These spires take centuries to grow, and you are wrecking them in a single day as you bumble this way and that! Why, Lochlan didn't snap this much coral in an entire year!"

Gray ground his teeth together. Takiza had brought up the name Lochlan *many* times since his training began. Apparently, Lochlan had been a favourite student of Takiza's and was now the leader of AuzyAuzy Shiver.

Takiza even called him "*my golden apprentice*"! Though he had never met the shark, Gray couldn't help disliking him. Muck-sucking teacher's pet, he thought.

"Again, Nulo!"

"Yes, Shiro!" Gray answered. "Shiro" meant *teacher* and *master* in some ancient language. Takiza insisted on being called this when they were training. Gray was "Nulo", which was a combination of *student* and *nothing*. He began swimming the course again.

On the second day of training, Gray had thrown a fit and tried to leave. Takiza didn't let him. "You gave your word to me," the betta told him. "Once accepted, it is not yours to take back!" Gray would never fight the little fish – Takiza had saved everyone's life at the Tuna Run – but instead he started swimming away.

Big mistake.

Takiza had dragged him back by the tail, commenting, "This is for your own good. It hurts me much more than you!" Somehow Gray doubted that. When he made the mistake of struggling, Takiza spun him around until he threw up! That was the last of Gray's rebellions.

"Can't we take a little break?" Gray asked now. "I'm tired."

"No, you are not. Megalodon do not tire so easily."

Gray stopped, flabbergasted. "You know I'm a megalodon?"

The betta flicked his fins in annoyance but answered, "It's as plain as the overly large snout on your face. I also know you were put in the Big Blue as a force for change. You are special, but if you rely on your gifts without seeking to improve yourself, you will fail. And you cannot fail!"

"Put here by who? Do you know my parents? What gifts do I have? And why can't I fail?"

"No questions, Nulo! They are unimportant at this moment! What *is* important is obeying what I tell you to do!"

Gray felt his voice go up, and he whined, "But I'm hungry and scraped by the coral, Takiza – I mean, Shiro. I don't want to be special. All I want to do is eat and sleep!"

The betta flicked his fins again as his eyes blazed. "You complain endlessly! You are soft and coddled, whining like a vain puffer fish at the merest discomfort. And you have no idea whatsoever of your true potential. Now swim the course or I will once again thrash you!"

Gray forced his aching tail to stroke left and right. He wouldn't get any answers right now, and he didn't want to be spun around again. Gaining speed, Gray used the wickedly cold and fast currents to his advantage just like the betta had shown him the day before.

These currents had a heaviness the ones above lacked. It was tougher to get in or out of these as the water flowed through the coral spire field and fell downwards towards the Dark Blue. Takiza had told him this was because water heading down had an entirely different weight and thickness. Lighter and thinner currents moved upwards, while the heavier ones travelled downwards. Takiza also said that all currents, no matter if they felt level or not, moved in one direction or the other, rising or falling. This was how the Big Blue cleansed itself, apparently.

Gray only knew it was hard to swim here.

Coral spires whizzed by on the left and right. Gray twisted and turned, instinctively leaving a heavy current that was rushing too fast over the edge and sliding into a slower one to brake himself without actually using his fins or tail.

"Excellent!" Takiza said, swimming upside down in front of his left eye. "Use your lateral line to feel the obstacles in your path."

The lateral line was another amazing thing Takiza had taught him. It was that buzzing feeling Gray got inside his head when he couldn't see but knew something was there. Sharkkind used it instinctively to hunt, Takiza had said. But to truly master it, you needed to practise and exercise its power.

"Don't rely on your eyes or your nose! Both can be fooled," the betta commented as he deftly dodged a thick rope of greenie. Gray's weight snapped it, and Takiza shook his head. "Never swim through things you can avoid."

"But, Shiro," Gray said, panting. The water felt thick pumping through his gills. "If I can go *through* something, isn't it faster because I'm swimming in a straight line?"

The frilly fish nodded, thinking. "That is true, except for . . ." Takiza trailed off as he adjusted his position upwards.

"Except for what?" Gray wheezed, just before smashing snout first into a giant coral spire, which didn't give at all. For a second, he was paralysed with pain, the current pushing his back and tail up against the coral.

Takiza shook his head and nudged Gray's stunned body into an area where the current wasn't about to sweep him off the ledge and into the Maw. "*Except for* the inevitable fact you will lose any time you have saved when striking an object thicker than even your very thick head, Nulo!"

Gray saw glowing motes swimming and winking everywhere. "Pretty," he mumbled, before taking a much-needed nap.

CHAPTER 14

THE CURRENT FLOWED BRISKLY ACROSS THE battle waters, which were very clear today. Whalem gave the orders for the armada to make the last of its preparations. Indi's mariners were massed on the south side of the Riptide territory. Apparently, the leader here had renamed the ancient shiver after himself, but that didn't matter. According to Indi Shiver, these were the Riptide homewaters. The terraced area, full of different single-colour greenie, was in the distance with Riptide Shiver sharks in a loose battle formation in front of that. Whalem could see their mariners were nervous, fins flicking and tails swishing. His stomach turned, sensing another oncoming slaughter. There was no glory in this. None at all.

Whalem noticed the industrious court shark Tydal making his own preparations in the floating royal court. Whalem disliked the court with all its pomp and vanity, but after this victory Finnivus could rightly call himself emperor of the seven seas. The arrogant tiger would want an elaborate ceremony, of course, hence Tydal's activity.

The past year had been wearing for Whalem. Seeing Finnivus grow more capricious and cruel with each victory sickened his stomach. He hoped his nausea was due to the slightly different fish of the Atlantis, but doubted it. Maybe, just maybe, after Finnivus had conquered everything he would calm down and rule well. Whalem felt a wave of despair as a small voice inside him whispered, "That won't happen. He'll become a monster."

"Why the long faces?" Finnivus boomed.

Whalem snapped to attention at his position by the lanternfish signaller and was relieved to find he wasn't the focus of the king's attention. It was a couple of young sharks from the Line. "This is my day! Everyone should be as happy, but never happier, than us!" Finnivus laughed his grating, high-pitched and ridiculous laugh.

A couple of the younglings had asked Finnivus if *they* could command the armada for the final battle instead of Whalem, but they were denied. That was the reason for their sour mood. Whalem didn't actually care and took the insulting request in his stride. He could have asked for single combat as was his right, but he had tired of all the blood being spilled. The more Whalem thought about the request, the more he realized it was a carefully laid trap. He was fifty summers older than the pups who'd challenged him. Victory would have been no sure thing, even with his combat experience. In any case, Finnivus was superstitious and insisted that everything stay the same.

Of course, the new royal herald would be the first to approach the other shiver. Finnivus cackled as the poor shark made what would in all likelihood be his last few tail strokes across the empty expanse between the mighty Indi armada and its pitiful opponents. Riptide had barely a hundred sharkkind.

Finnivus motioned at the herald with a fin and told the court, "He's going to say that their leader has to admit he is a jelly-brained turtle next to my glorious magnificence! Ha!" More high-pitched laughing.

Whalem, in his position off to the side, could not hear the herald as he delivered the message and waited for what he knew was certain death. Heralds weren't allowed to defend themselves. Their job was to wait for a reply. That the reply could be – today more than ever – a bite to the gills was beside the point.

Curiously, the mako leader of Riptide Shiver listened to everything and didn't attack the herald, which would have undoubtedly begun the battle. Indeed, she – the leader looked female even from this distance – seemed to be answering. After a moment, the herald swam back towards the king's court!

What was this?

"Tydal!" shouted Finnivus. "Why aren't we fighting?

Why is there no killing?" The king adjusted himself on one of his blue whales.

"I'm – I'm not sure, Your Magnificence," the epaulette shark stammered. Tydal's fins seemed to move in opposite directions and at cross purposes.

"Find out this instant!" Finnivus yelled.

Tydal swam as fast as he could from his position in the court to the approaching herald. Whalem followed. He could signal his lanternfish and have the Indi armada in action at a moment's notice, but he wanted to hear this.

"I greet you, First Court Fish –" the herald began. The official greeting between them would last far too long and Tydal knew it.

"Forget all that!" the epaulette whispered urgently. "What's happening?"

"She agreed."

"By Tyro's tail, make sense!" Tydal urged, his own tail twitching as if he were being shocked by an eel.

"Their leader wants me to deliver a message to the king that she'll do everything he demands," the herald told him.

Whalem's heart leapt. Could the day end with *none* of his mariners swimming the Sparkle Blue? It seemed too good to be true. Tydal was caught open-mouthed, gills pumping spastically. All he could do was ask, "Really?"

"What's happening, Tydal?" shouted Finnivus from his throne. "We grow agitated and not amused!"

A split-second decision was needed. In the deadly world of royal mood swings, it could mean Tydal's life. "Deliver the message," he heard the court shark say.

This was about to get interesting. Tydal took his place in the court as the herald explained. It was for the king's ears only, so no one else could hear. Heralds were taught this skill; they could speak loudly enough for thousands to hear, or quietly enough so only one would, even in a crowd.

After listening, Finnivus laughed with glee, bouncing himself on the back of the blue whale underneath him. For once, Whalem thought, the ridiculous laugh was the most welcome sound in all the Big Blue. "Excellent! Bring their leader to me this instant!"

The commander of the *squaline* ordered the king's personal guards to form a defensive line. Another complement of mariners circled above the king, protecting his dorsal. These armoured guards were faster than all but a few unarmoured sharks, which was why they'd been chosen for this duty.

The prisoner swam up slowly, pressed flank to flank between two massive great white *squaline*, so she couldn't streak into an attack. The mako leader of Riptide Shiver was beautiful, there was no denying that.

"I'm honoured to hover in the presence of the wise and mighty Finnivus Victor," she said, loud enough for everyone in the royal court to hear. "I'll happily swim to the Sparkle Blue today because I've met the greatest shark in all the oceans and seas!" She smiled and showed her thin and pointed teeth in a friendly way.

"And what do they call you?" asked Finnivus.

"My name is Velenka, Your Magnificence."

Finnivus smiled at the court, which hung on his every word. "She certainly is well-mannered for an uncultured fish." He tittered at his own joke, immediately joined by everyone else.

Velenka then said, "Your Majesty's laugh is a most beautiful music."

Whalem's opinion of the Riptide leader changed immediately. This shark *was* a threat, but not to him or Finnivus. She was a threat to anyone in court who would fight for rank with her.

One youngling in the Line realized this immediately, too. "Make her wish come true, Majesty!" he yelled. "Feast on her! The leader of the last ancient shiver in the Big Blue would make a fitting meal to announce the age of *Emperor* Finnivus!"

Finnivus preened for the mako and made a show of thinking about this. But Whalem knew she was too beautiful and too interesting for the king to resist. Finnivus clicked his notched teeth together. "I really should eat you. If there isn't going to be a battle for my amusement, then I should have you for dinner to celebrate. My fourth is right about that."

"An emperor does what he wants," Velenka said calmly.

"In the end his word is law, no matter what anyone else thinks."

Whalem almost shook his head in amazement. What an answer! Now if Finnivus were to order the mako's death, it would seem based on someone else's advice, which would make him look weak.

Amazingly, he seemed even more interested. "But surely blood must be spilled on our glorious day!" Finnivus replied. "What would you have me do?"

Whalem almost spun around in surprise. Finnivus was asking someone else for an opinion!

The mako performed a graceful bow and cast her eyes downwards. It was as if she'd been born at court. "Emperor, Riptide Shiver is no more. Every sharkkind formerly a part of it is yours to do with as you wish."

"Oh, I'd like to destroy every one of your puny mariners, but undoubtedly Whalem would feel terrible about it." The gathered court fins laughed. Finnivus continued, "But you've been so charming, it would be a shame to eat you. How about your Line? Will you feast on them with me and prove your loyalty?"

The sunlight caught Velenka's pitch-black upper half, and a rainbow reflected from it. "They are as loyal to me as I will be to you, Emperor. My Line would be honoured to sacrifice themselves for your celebration."

"Then come, let's go for a swim while the royal seasoners do their work, then. You can show me around my newest homewaters."

"I am honoured," she told Finnivus.

Whalem swam off, as his part in the day was over. And honoured or not, there was a good deal of screaming when it became clear to the sharkkind in the Riptide Line what was in store for them.

CHAPTER 15

VELENKA SWAM THROUGH THE RIPTIDE homewaters at the flank of the soon-to-be emperor of the Big Blue. He was at least five or six seasons younger than she was. Velenka could only dream of having the power he was born into. The way was now clear for him to impose his will on all the seven seas. She knew there was a whale of a difference between a regular shiver and a royal shiver, and she struggled to remember her lessons on the subject. She adjusted her position so that her snout wouldn't surpass the tiger's front flipper. Position and appearances were *everything* in a royal court. *That* she did remember.

"I see that this shiver did a little seascaping," Finnivus told her. "It's nothing like my, umm, *our* homewaters, but it's the best we've seen in the Atlantis."

Velenka almost laughed at the pup king's mistakes using the royal *we*. But laughing wouldn't have been wise. Velenka escorted him through the Riptide home-waters proper, and he wasn't entirely disdainful, especially after he saw the terraced greenie gardens with their bright, bright colours.

"Not terrible," he commented.

Velenka risked a sidelong peek at the tiger. Was Finnivus a conqueror supreme? Or a spoiled brat who'd got lucky?

"I can't take credit for the terraces," she told him. "I was only leader for a few days before you arrived."

"Really? How did that happen?"

That was an open question. A very *smart* open question. Finnivus hadn't offered a clue about what he was thinking, or what he might like her to say. The sleek tattooed tiger shark was much sharper than Goblin, that was for sure.

"Our leader went missing," Velenka said, keeping her fins perfectly still. She didn't want to seem nervous. "Either he saw your armada and swam away in fright, or . . . he died of a jellyfish sting. There are different rumours."

Finnivus laughed. The high-pitched chortle was almost comical. "He died of a jellyfish sting just before I would have eaten him? Not likely! He ran and hid like a little turtle hatchling!"

"If he *was* sent to the Sparkle Blue by a jelly, maybe the drifters also want you to be their emperor."

Finnivus fell silent. For a moment Velenka thought

that she had overplayed her hand, but then he laughed. "Oh, that's too good!" he chortled. "*Drifters* wanting me to be emperor! You have a keen wit!"

The laughter spread to the surrounding court sharks, which once again reminded Velenka that they weren't alone. Of course, royalty should have a retinue, but this was ridiculous. There were at least twenty-five sharkkind constantly within three or four tail strokes of Finnivus at all times. Plus, his personal guard was there, coated in metallic skin. They swam so quietly, it was a miracle she could hear them at all. And a mere tail's length away was the first court shark, a brown-and-yellow epaulette. Velenka ignored him completely as did everyone else. Then there were the young sharkkind of the Line who eyed her balefully. There were also many other sharks and dwellers whose jobs and names she didn't know. Velenka would learn everything about them as if her life depended on it.

Which was undoubtedly truer than she knew.

"Yes, yes," Finnivus said to himself as he looked around at the colourful greenie bordering the ancient Speakers Rock at the centre of the Riptide homewaters. "This place is the most worthy we've seen. Tydal, my ceremony shall be here. Make the preparations. And do tell us when our meal is ready."

The epaulette shark bobbed his head. "At once, Magnificence!" Tydal did an eel-quick turn and vanished. Finnivus gave her a grin. "He's good at what he does."

"Oh, I'm sure he is, Your Majesty," Velenka said. "I'd

only expect the most gifted sharkkind to be allowed near you."

"Yes, you'd *expect* that," he said, casting a sidelong glance at an older tiger shark with intricate tattoos. Velenka wondered if she, too, would have to get tattoos. They didn't look half bad. The black wave pattern was quite striking, but the ones the royalty wore were even better. Finnivus continued, "But sometimes you don't have a choice in the matter."

The shark in question seemed to be the mariner prime who led the battle armada. The young sharkkind in the Line joined with their king to laugh at this not-so-private joke. The older tiger, obviously not someone to be trifled with, acted as if he hadn't heard anything.

"You have proved yourself most interesting," Finnivus commented. Velenka bobbed her head and cast her eyes downwards as she had seen the court shark do. How she hated scraping before anyone, even royalty. "I want you in court for my coronation ceremony."

Velenka acted flustered even though this was what she'd been hoping for secretly. "I – I don't know what to say, Your Majesty. Such an honour! You're such a kind and compassionate ruler to a poor fin you've just conquered!"

Finnivus preened as if Velenka was stroking his underbelly. In a way, she was. It didn't matter. She needed to stay close to the pup if she were to survive.

"We are kind and compassionate to all who, umm, *we* rule."

Even more rewarding to Velenka than the invitation was the look of absolute horror on the faces of the sharks of the Line. One female spinner shark even gnashed her teeth.

Velenka started when the court shark Tydal announced, "Dinner is served, Your Majesty," right behind her. Apparently, the little muck-sucker could sneak around with the best of them.

"Ah, excellent," Finnivus said. "Lead us, Tydal."

They swam back to Speakers Rock in front of the terraces of coloured greenie. Already, Velenka could see that the dwellers in Indi Shiver were decorating the area in their colours for the coronation.

In all the excitement Velenka had forgotten that they would be dining on her Line. Some of it, anyway. Ripper, the battle-scarred hammerhead and the first of Goblin Shiver, hadn't returned from a long-range patrol. Maybe he'd been killed by an Indi patrol. Ripper was a lucky one, then. At least he had died in battle.

Velenka looked at the faces of her ex-shivermates arranged on a rock disc carried on the backs of four sea turtles. Not to eat would be counted against her. The young sharks of Indi's court certainly thought so. They dug in with Finnivus but kept looking over, eagerly waiting for Velenka to say she couldn't join them.

"Not hungry?" asked Finnivus. This was another test, of course. The young tiger was devious, all right.

"Nonsense, Your Majesty," she told Finnivus loudly enough for everyone to hear. "I'm starving!"

Halfway through the meal, Velenka discovered it wasn't so bad. In fact, Streak was kind of tasty.

CHAPTER 16

"SETTLE DOWN!" SHOUTED QUICKEYES, THE thresher leader of Coral Shiver. "I don't want to be a hard shell, but we need to stop talking over each other!" It had been six hours since Gray and the rest of Rogue Shiver had passed the Rock Lobster formation and entered Coral Shiver's hidden homewaters. He had just swum back from training with Takiza yesterday and thankfully had been able to get a good sleep in before an emergency council meeting was called.

"He's right," Sandy said. "Let's weigh up our options."

It suddenly became quiet enough to hear a couple of minnows darting around above their heads. Gray was once again awed by his mother. She stayed calm and cool when everyone else was tumbling around in the current. Coral Shiver was evenly split on whether they should stay or move because of the danger Indi Shiver posed. Solutions were scarce and the arguments on each side grew more and more heated. Since Rogue and Coral Shivers had formally agreed to join together soon after their introduction by Gray, both Lines could speak their minds. That was why this particular council meeting was so raucous. It wasn't just five opinions – it was ten!

"If we left here, where would we go?" Mari asked, loud enough to be heard. She made a circle with her long tail. "Indi Shiver's territory is now the *entire* Big Blue!"

It was a good point. There were grumbles and murmurs from both sides.

"I say we stay and fight!" Striiker announced, gnashing his triangular teeth. Of course he did. It didn't take much for the great white to get himself in an uproar. What was surprising was that Onyx completely supported him. The blacktip and Striiker had become fast friends. They were very much alike, as both sometimes let their tempers get the best of them.

"He's making good sense," Onyx told everyone. "This royal brat will have to get his snout bloodied before he learns his lesson!"

"You can't be serious, Onyx," Barkley remarked, rolling his eyes. "You've seen how Indi Shiver fights. And they outnumber us at least twenty to one!"

"And that's just what's here today," Shell added. "They could bring more. A lot more."

"Yes," Quickeyes agreed. "You're probably right."

113

Onyx's tail drooped. He brushed the sandy bottom of the seabed, raising a cloud of sand. "Doesn't mean we have to like it." Unlike Striiker, once Onyx thought things through, he was more likely to come to a wise decision. Gray hoped the great white would learn this skill one day.

"Is there a place to go where there are less of them?" asked Snork. "A place that Indi sharks don't like?"

"If they don't like it, we probably wouldn't, either," Sandy told the sawfish. "What we have in common far outweighs our differences."

"But we're not eating the seasoned heads of everyone we meet," Shell said in his understated way.

Earlier in the day, Onyx had infiltrated Indi Shiver as a hunter. Since the blacktip wore their tattoos, he'd been able to get away with it, and even brought back a few fish. Onyx had heard many things about Finnivus. Unfortunately, none of them were good.

Gray pondered. "Maybe they'll leave soon. Like the other places you heard they had conquered."

Onyx nodded. "The word around camp is that Finnivus hates everything that isn't the Indi homewaters."

"So that's good," said Mari.

"No. They'll leave a force of mariners to hold the territory," Barkley noted. "Or what's the point of conquering anything?"

"But a holding force would be smaller and easier to avoid, or fight, than this armada," Sandy countered.

"The least dangerous course of action seems to be to hide and wait."

"Hide and wait, hide and wait," Striiker blurted. "That's all you ever want to do!"

Gray was about to come to his mother's defence, but she stopped him with the twitch of a fin. She could fight her own battles. "Sometimes that's the smart thing to do, Striiker. Never let your pride get you into a fight. Especially one you can't win."

The great white caught Gray glaring at him over his mother's dorsal and didn't argue.

"Okay, I've heard enough," said Quickeyes. The thresher looked around the gathered sharkkind. Various dwellers waited to see what, if anything, would be decided. "Coral Shiver will stay and keep our snouts in the greenie for now. If Rogue wants to leave – of course they can. We'll quietly search for other homewaters while we're waiting this out. One that's further away from the Riptide territory and more defensible." It was easy for Quickeyes to use the name Riptide. He had never known it as Goblin Shiver.

Shell looked to Gray. "What do you think?"

As Rogue Shiver's leader, Gray had to make his thoughts known to his own Line. "It's the best plan for now. If something changes, or anyone wants to leave, come talk with me."

"And the training?" Striiker asked. Coral Shiver sharks, even pups, were being taught by Striiker and

Onyx to fight. This had never been done before, but sadly, now it was needed.

"The training should continue," Gray told everyone.

But what good would the out-of-date drills they had learned from Goblin do against Indi Shiver? Not much. Gray guessed that something was better than nothing. Just not a lot better.

The shiver council meeting ended with everyone drifting off in twos and threes. Quickeyes swam over to Gray just as he was about to get a few words alone with his mother.

"You didn't say too much during the meeting," the thresher told him.

"I didn't have anything important to add," Gray answered sheepishly.

"Listening usually beats talking. Most fins don't learn that until they're much older than you." Quickeyes glanced at Striiker, who was having an energetic argument with Mari and Barkley. "Or not at all."

"Give him a chance," Gray told Coral's leader. "It takes a while to get used to his . . . let's say, colourful personality, but Striiker's loyal."

Quickeyes nodded at the comment and gave Sandy a look. "He really has grown up and done you proud." He waggled a fin at Gray. "How's it going with Takiza?"

"You remember how mad I used to make you and everyone else? It's a good day when I only make him *that* mad."

Sandy and Quickeyes chuckled. The thresher swished his long tail once and swam off. "Please keep us informed about what you're doing."

Gray got to catch up with his mother then. For a little while, it was just the two of them and that was great. For some reason being with his mum made him feel like everything was going to turn out all right. Gray knew his feelings wouldn't do him any good in a real fight – then he'd rather have Striiker at his flank – but it was nice.

Barkley and Mari came over. Barkley gestured at Striiker talking with Onyx. "That great white chowderhead tires me out just listening. I'm so glad Quickeyes is more like you, Sandy."

"Thanks for the compliment, Barkley, but the truth is, Striiker and Onyx are right."

"What!" Barkley exclaimed a little too loudly. Striiker and Onyx stared for a moment but then went back to their energetic conversation. The dogfish lowered his voice. "You can't be serious. Their type of thinking will get us killed."

"What do you mean, Mum?" Gray asked. Mari swam closer so she could hear everything.

"We won't be able to feed the shiver with just a few of us quietly hunting," Gray's mother explained. "This type of living has a time limit. We either find a place that's safe – something that might not exist if Indi Shiver tightens their grip on the major hunting territories – or we have to face them."

"They may still go back to their own homewaters," Mari added, but without much conviction.

Barkley knew Sandy was right and was dismayed. "We can't win. I saw them fight. We can't!"

Mari bumped the dogfish's flank. "Quit bringing us down, Barkley. We're safe and all together right now. Let's be happy about that."

Barkley nodded. "You're right. And who knows? Maybe Takiza will teach Gray a few tricks, and he'll beat up their armada all by himself!"

"Yeah, right," Gray said as he gave his friend a good-natured tail slap. "Or maybe you and Yappy can just talk them to death."

"Did someone say my name?" shouted Yappy. "You guys done with your big meeting? We had one, too! During our meeting a sea cucumber scared Prime Minister Shocks. Can you believe that? They move so slowly, and still, Shocks got scared! Ha! Hey, where do you think sea cucumbers come from?"

Barkley looked at Gray with a mock-annoyed expression. "This is your fault."

Mari snorted, and Snork also came over, swimming low and digging through the greenie with his long saw bill, looking for treats. The topics of the ensuing conversation were many and varied. Gray, Barkley, Mari and Sandy said nothing. They just relaxed, and for this night, tried to forget their troubles.

It didn't work for Gray, though. He knew that soon, someone – or more likely an armada of someones – would have to swim out and face Finnivus and his black wave of mariners.

THE
CORONATION

CHAPTER 17

WHALEM'S SPINE ACHED, AS IT DID FROM TIME to time. Remaining stock-still, at the hover – as Finnivus's coronation ceremony required – was the absolute worst! Injuries from battles fought in his younger days were calcifying and growing stiff with his advanced years. And performing the attention hover added greatly to Whalem's spinal pain. It was difficult to hold for long periods of time, and he had ordered the armada to assume this position almost an hour ago. Whalem heard the groans of his mariners only in his mind as they were too disciplined to express their discomfort out loud. Now, what they were thinking was another matter.

There wasn't a thing he could do to slow the tide of old age, but following the royal doctor fish's advice to stretch and bend each morning did help. Whalem had also used that time to ask Tyro to give Finnivus the understanding of his almost limitless power and the wisdom never to use it.

So far, either Tyro wasn't hearing him, or Finnivus wasn't listening to Tyro.

The current strengthened slightly. Whalem moved his tail fins in almost imperceptible strokes to hold his position stock-still in relation to Finnivus's throne. Oh, how he wished the ceremony would end!

Whalem knew it was an insult for him not to be next to the other royal sharks in the court. One of his commanders, or even a subcommander, could very ably have led the armada in attention hover. Whalem almost chuckled, picturing Finnivus trying to maintain attention hover for even five minutes. The spoiled pup had never known a day when he wasn't waited on snout and fin. If the royal seasoners didn't place food directly in his mouth, Finnivus might starve in the open ocean.

Tydal, the epaulette court shark, glided down a track of brilliant red and blue crabs underneath him. Thankfully, it seemed that the ceremony was coming to its important part. Tydal stopped smartly and began to recite the words that would declare Finnivus emperor. By coincidence, a bitter cold current flowed through the area.

Staying in formation was now complete agony! Whalem willed Tydal to hurry. The little epaulette shark did do his job well. From negotiating with the nearby whales to form a choir, to changing what had been Riptide Shiver's homewaters over to Indi colours, everything looked very regal.

In a steady and clear voice, Tydal began the final proclamation. Surely, the first court shark must know that the slightest mistake here would guarantee his shrieking death. But the epaulette went on, smooth and steady. "Whereas it pleased Tyro to call our glorious King Romulus Victor to the Sparkle Blue and replace him with his even more glorious son Finnivus Victor, we are awed and inspired to acknowledge that his kingly rank must be raised due to his numerous magnificent accomplishments!"

The soon-to-be emperor squealed and giggled in delight as the battles of the Indi armada now became exaggerated tales. For example, in the Arktik, the armada hadn't even seen a single orca, but that campaign was now called the Destruction of Icingholme Shiver Homewaters and Its Mighty Orckic Battle Pods.

Tydal went on, "So the good fins of the Big Blue acknowledge and recognize that through his mastery of the martial arts and uncountable victories, King Finnivus Victor shall be hereby and forever known as Emperor Finnivus Victor Triumphant, Conqueror of the Seven Seas and Overlord of the Four Oceans. All sharkkind and dwellers will bow before Finnivus Victor Triumphant!"

There was a muted *thwump* as every fin and dweller present did a communal head bob of deference. Whalem cast his eyes downwards and looked up at the eager new emperor, swishing his tail back and forth in excitement. Tydal shouted, "I give you Emperor of all the Waters, Finnivus Triumphant! ALL HAIL THE EMPEROR!"

The gathered crowd and armada responded, "HAIL! HAIL! LONG LIVE EMPEROR FINNIVUS VICTOR TRIUMPHANT!" Whalem moved his mouth but couldn't bring himself to say the words with any conviction. But it did give him a chance to ease out of the strict attention hover. He saw the armada take the same liberty and allowed it. After a moment, everyone relaxed. Finnivus and the royals in the court no longer cared about them. The armada was only in their minds when they were in danger or needed to conquer something. Otherwise, they didn't care a fin flick for any mariner's sacrifices.

Whalem had his commanders dismiss the armada. They could watch the festivities from a respectful distance or go and hunt or rest. He could see that the mariners who chose hunting or sleeping far outnumbered those who wanted to watch the emperor enjoy himself. Whalem began swimming away to get some sleep, but a *squaline* intercepted him.

"Mariner Prime, you are summoned to court to congratulate the Emperor Finnivus." Whalem followed the guard to where Finnivus held court. He was made to wait by another nervous *squaline*, who mumbled, "I am sorry, Mariner Prime. Orders."

"Do your duty," Whalem replied evenly, grinding his notched teeth in annoyance. Another insult.

Tydal saw this and darted over. "What are you doing? Don't you recognize the first in the Line of Indi Shiver and mariner prime of the armada?"

"Yes, sir, I do . . ." The guard looked over Tydal's shoulder and received a nod from the commander of the *squaline*. "Go right on through, sir. Very sorry."

Whalem swam towards Finnivus with Tydal at his side.

"I apologize Mariner Prime. I hadn't thought to check if – if something like that would happen."

"You had other things on your mind," Whalem responded.

Tydal nodded and went ahead to announce his arrival. Beside Finnivus was Velenka, the former leader of Riptide Shiver. Whalem could see the mako was already bumping snouts for position in the royal court. After Tydal spoke in a low voice to Finnivus, the emperor shouted across the homewaters, "Come, come! Whalem, my first! Where have you been?"

"With the armada, sir, as ancient protocol did dictate."

Finnivus grinned. "Oh, that! Pish-posh, you should have been here! Father would have insisted! You were friends, yes?"

Whalem's insides turned to stone. Finnivus knew

very well that he and Romulus had been like brothers. "Yes," he answered. "He would have insisted."

One of the pups from the Line saw an opening and pounced. "What do you mean? Are you saying that Emperor Finnivus wronged you in some way?"

The shocking falseness of the question caught Whalem by surprise. How could anyone doubt his loyalty? He should have immediately said something – become enraged at the smart-mouthed flipper – but was stunned into silence. He caught a glimpse of Finnivus, who instead of protesting the innocent mistake, *watched* Whalem like he was some sort of traitor!

"Should I have taken time on the day of my royal coronation as emperor of the entire Big Blue to make sure you came to the ceremony?" Finnivus asked mockingly, getting a laugh from the court.

"Of course not, Your Majesty," Whalem began. Then his emotions got the better of him, and he added, "But you could have sent someone." There was silence in the court.

"This is an outrage, Emperor!" someone yelled from the Line.

Finnivus looked down from his position over Speakers Rock and said, "We are not offended." But the emperor's words did not match the flat, dead look in his eyes. "You seem tired, Whalem. You are very old. Get some rest."

And there it was. He was dismissed.

As he left, Whalem caught Tydal watching. Of course, he couldn't tell what the court shark was thinking, unlike the pups of the Line who were absolutely giddy at his mistake. Whalem was mariner prime and first in the Line in name only now. How soon would his head be first in the line at the royal seasoners?

CHAPTER 18

GRAY AND TAKIZA WERE BACK AT THE TRAINING ground next to the Maw. It was pitch-black, for it was night above the chop-chop, with no moon to provide even a little light. The ancient coral spires stood, wickedly sharp and unmoving, mocking him in the darkness. The greenie harness chafed and rubbed Gray raw under his fins and belly. How Takiza had managed to weave it was a marvel. The frilly betta took a long strand of greenie in his mouth and looped through the water this way and that, almost faster than the eye could see. When it was done, Gray didn't know what to make of it. But now that the harness was on him, he knew exactly what it was – a torture device.

"Can I take a break, Shiro?"

Takiza released a frustrated whoosh of water from his gills. "You may loaf after you have mastered this exercise. Unfortunately, you have all the grace of a pregnant sea cow, and I despair of you ever completing this task."

Gray muttered under his breath, "I'll give you a pregnant sea cow . . ."

Takiza gave him a surprisingly strong tail slap across the snout. "What was that, Nulo?"

"Nothing, Shiro!"

"I know it was nothing. The vast majority of things you say are nothing. So stop muttering and concentrate! Now – again!"

Gray could hear the greenie in the harness stretch as he pulled the giant rock inside off the seabed. He navigated the course carefully, floating the rock between, over and under various obstacles. "Good, feel the weight and shape of the burden you are carrying. Use your lateral line to sense it as if it were an extension of your own pudgy body," Takiza said into his ear.

"I'm not pudgy, Shiro! Mum says I'm just big cartilaged," Gray answered through clenched teeth as he strained.

Another tail slap. "Quiet, Nulo! Your mother is a gentle soul who was merely being kind! Listen and learn!"

"Yeah, right," Gray said sarcastically. "Because I'm *sooo* special. But will you tell me why I'm special? Why I have to do this stuff? *Nooo*." He looked Takiza right in the eye, something that usually made the Siamese fighting fish act like his name.

Instead, his teacher sighed. "If I tell you some small

bit of what I know, will there be no more complaining for the rest of this session?"

Gray couldn't believe his luck! Maybe he'd just worn Takiza down! He found that hard to believe, but wasn't going to look a gift bluefin in the mouth. "Yes! I promise. No more complaining!"

"There is an ancient prophecy that tells of a great sharkkind leading every good fin in the ocean against an ancient evil."

"And?"

The little betta ruffled his fins. "And I have now told you one small bit of prophecy."

"But that could mean *anything*!" Gray whined. "And it could be for anyone!"

"Yes, it could. Frustrating, isn't it? That's why it's best not to put too much stock in prophecy. Now, I have kept my end of the bargain –"

"By tricking me!" Gray interrupted, whipping his tail back and forth to try and warm up.

Takiza shook his head. "Oh, if tricking you were less easy, your training would proceed much faster. I could never trick Lochlan, my golden apprentice. But you? Every time it gets easier. Come, Nulo, swim!"

Lochlan, Lochlan, Lochlan! The golden wonder shark! Gray couldn't wait to one day meet this teacher's pet and bop him right in the snout for being such a goody-goody.

Gray forced himself forward. The little betta loved

talking during training, and it usually broke Gray's concentration. Maybe that was part of the lesson. If Gray could manage to listen and understand what was being said even through a flurry of insults, then his concentration would improve.

Or maybe Takiza just liked insulting him.

"Feel the distance between the rock and the ocean floor. Feel how you are now *dragging* the rock in the sand, instead of properly floating it as I told you."

Gray strained against the harness and adjusted his depth so the rock was off the seabed. It wasn't so bad after he got going, but lifting off was tough.

"Feel the currents around you. Use them to your advantage. Work with the ocean, not against it."

"I *am* working with it," Gray huffed, gills pumping furiously from his efforts. "But it doesn't want to work with *me*!" Nevertheless, he floated the rock underneath the hardest portion of the course, a low ceiling formed by a fallen coral spire. One that Gray hadn't broken. It was fiendishly tricky to keep the rock moving forward as there was only a tail length between his dorsal fin and the urchin spine – sharp coral above, and an equally short distance between the seabed and the bottom of the harnessed rock below. If the rock hit the ocean floor, as it had all ten times Gray had tried today, it was impossible to get enough lift in the cramped area to get moving again. But this time, with some skill and a favourable current...

"Ha! I did it!" Gray said, swishing his tail with a flourish. "Take that, obstacle course!"

Takiza nodded. "Finally, one small victory. Of course, Lochlan did it on his first try. Have I mentioned that if you could be somewhat like him, your training would go much faster?"

"You may have said that once or twice, Shiro."

"Good. Now we can practise at a greater depth, my young apprentice."

Gray groaned. He couldn't imagine carrying the rock in the harness while struggling to breathe in the Dark Blue. He was about to object when Takiza did a quick half loop and plunged into the sand.

"What have we here?" asked the betta, bouncing a large sandy rock with his gauzy tailfin. "Explain yourself this instant!"

Gray thought Takiza had gone crazy, ordering a stone to speak. Then he saw it wasn't a rock at all. "Trank! What are you doing here?"

But the stonefish didn't answer. Or move. From the shocked look in his eyes, it appeared Takiza had paralysed him with one of his mysterious pressure-point fin touches. When Gray asked to learn the move, Takiza laughed as if it were the funniest thing he'd ever heard.

"You know this stonefish? Do you realize his kind are quite low in character? And this particular one seems even lower than most."

"He's okay," Gray said. "Let him go."

Takiza sighed. "Very well." The frilly betta did a quick turn around the floating stonefish and touched him with a fin flick between the eyes.

Trank's fins began moving. He backed away from the betta and closer to Gray. "That's a neat trick, Takiza. It is Takiza, isn't it?"

"It is."

"I'm sure Gafin would pay if youse would teach that to a few of us."

"Gafin would, would he?" Takiza gave the stonefish a smirk. "Tell Gafin to make the offer to me in person."

"Gafin don't see no one."

"In that case we are at an impasse."

"What are you doing here, Trank?" Gray asked again.

The stonefish was still mad about being paralysed. It took him a few seconds before he could answer. "You know you're behind on what youse owe us?"

Takiza snorted derisively.

Trank gave him a look but went on. "Gafin knows yer good for it, but keep it in mind."

"First day off I have, I promise to go to hunting for you."

"Okay, fine," the stonefish said. "Then there is one other thing." Trank paused before continuing, his eyes darting between Gray and Takiza. "Velenka wants to meet."

"No," Takiza said, shaking his head. "That one swims with Indi Shiver now."

"She does?" Gray said in surprise.

Trank eyed Takiza suspiciously. "How do youse know that?"

The frilly betta ignored the question. "It is a trap," Takiza told Gray matter-of-factly.

"Gafin gives his word for your safety inside Slagger-nacks."

"What about *outside*?" asked the betta.

"Show Gafin some respect!" the stonefish growled. "Velenka knows we can get to her if she doesn't play nice. If she and I can do business, you can, too."

"It's dangerous to trust Velenka," Gray said to himself. "And Barkley would kill me."

"Finally, you prove there is something other than chowder in that huge head of yours," Takiza commented.

Trank swam closer to Gray. "Yeah, she thought youse wouldn't just come for a snack and the band, so she said to tell youse what it's about."

"Which is?"

"It's about Coral Shiver's continued safety, she says." Takiza swam around Trank very slowly, and the stone-fish began spinning as if he were caught in a whirlpool. "Hey, stop it! Stop it!"

The betta ignored Trank and spoke to Gray. "If she knew where your family was, Velenka would have already traded that information to secure her position with the emperor."

"Hey! This isn't funny!" shouted the now wildly spinning Trank.

But the way Gray saw it, there was no choice. "I can't take the chance, Shiro. I have to go."

Takiza sighed. "You are an extremely troublesome apprentice, Nulo. Not like Lochlan at all."

CHAPTER 19

IT HAD TAKEN GRAY TWO DAYS TO SWIM BACK to Coral Shiver from the training grounds because the current was running against him. He stopped by Slaggernacks and left word that he would meet with Velenka. Then, after making sure no one was following, Gray swam to Coral's temporary homewaters. The shiver was safe, and Quickeyes promised to suspend all feeding while Gray went to his meeting. Every shark in the shiver would have to ignore their rumbling bellies for a while. They couldn't take the chance of being spotted. Onyx, Barkley, Mari and the rest would continue searching for another, more defensible, place they could move to in case they were discovered. But how many times could Coral Shiver run?

After picking off a few oily mackerel, Gray crept through the dense greenie until he got to the edge of the field and stopped. He surveyed the maze of rocky caverns, coral and greenie, whose jumble formed Slaggernacks. How could this odd place have become so important? It was still supposedly neutral ground, but only because Emperor Finnivus and Indi Shiver didn't know it existed. Would it still be safe once they found out about it? The Indi armada was a power unlike any the Big Blue had seen in a thousand years. What were a few poisonous dwellers compared to that?

Everyone in Rogue Shiver and quite a few in Coral had offered to back up Gray for his meeting with Velenka. But Gray made the decision as Rogue Shiver leader that no one else could come, something he had never done. There was no way he wanted others risking their lives. For the safety of both Rogue and Coral Shivers, he needed to do this by himself. If Velenka's information helped, that was good. If it was a trap, well, then Gray would be the only one caught.

Trank had given his word, but was his word to be trusted? Gray felt a cold tingle creep down his spine that had nothing to do with the coming of winter and the water cooling. He looked into the distance around Slaggernacks and saw nothing unusual. He even tried to reach out with his *other* senses that Takiza was constantly berating him to use. Sometimes when Gray used his lateral line, there was a faint electrical buzzing when he located another sharkkind or fish. But now he felt no other presence aside from the usual small dwellers going about their lives. Gnashing his teeth nervously a few times, Gray swam towards the back caverns.

Trank floated upwards from a pile of rocks near some waving greenie. "Didn't know if youse would show."

Not for the first time, Gray wondered how many of the rocks near Slaggernacks were actually stonefish, or something equally venomous in disguise.

"Am I the first?" he asked. He'd arrived an hour before he was supposed to so he could be in the cave before Velenka.

Gray was dismayed when Trank answered, "Youse wish. Watch your back."

"Not coming in?"

Trank shook his head, causing a cloud of dirt to fall from his seemingly malformed scales. How stonefish could live like that, Gray didn't know. "She wanted privacy and paid a large amount to get everyone out. Youse is on your own."

Gray swam cautiously into the smallish cavern. Glowing coral grew only sparsely here. Without lumos to provide light, it was nearly black. But now his lateral line buzzed. Gray could feel Velenka's position clearly. He took a quick look at the craggy ceiling of the cave and saw that it was bare; there were no poisonous urchins or octos. As Trank had said, they were alone.

"Gray, it's good to see you," said Velenka, rolling her mako tail and giving him a smile. Her upper half almost merged with the gloom around them. Those eyes – they seemed even more disconcertingly black now. Gray shivered involuntarily. Once he had liked being around Velenka. But now, despite her beauty and brains, it was as if darkness oozed from her very being.

"What do you want, Velenka?"

The mako winced exaggeratedly. "No hello? No, 'I'm glad the emperor didn't kill you'?"

"How can you deal with being around that maniac?" Gray asked.

"Finnivus isn't a maniac! He's misunderstood!" she said with sudden intensity. "I have to get close to him."

"Convenient for you."

"Convenient for everyone!" she shouted. Her voice rang off the stone ceiling. "The emperor will destroy you if he's not managed."

"And you're just the shark to do that."

"With your help," Velenka answered quietly.

Gray couldn't believe it. She was asking him to trust her? After she had betrayed him and his friends on more than one occasion? "I'll trust you – after *Goblin* tells me it's okay to do that." There were rumours that Goblin hadn't been at the face-off with Indi Shiver. It was very suspicious that the stubborn and aggressive great white leader had disappeared so completely.

Velenka bristled. "I'm the only hope the sharkkind and dwellers around here have! That includes your mother!"

Gray rammed the mako, pinning her against the wall

with his bulk. He was sure this was painful, but he didn't care. "Don't – don't you talk about my mum."

"Goblin was a fool," she hissed. "He was going to get us all killed! I had to act!"

"Tell me what you know!" Gray yelled. Then he eased up. When it came to it, Gray couldn't just bite Velenka and send her to the Sparkle Blue.

"He's going to search the area carefully for any hidden shivers," she told him. "That's what Indi always does after they beat the main forces. They'll crush anyone they find. It teaches a lesson to everyone who might want to make trouble after they've left for their homewaters. This way Finnivus can leave a smaller force to hold this area."

"But have they found Coral Shiver yet?"

From the glint in Velenka's eye, Gray knew he'd made a mistake. His heart sank as she said, "So they *are* still here."

She hadn't known until just now, he thought. Until I opened my big, fat mouth. Gray tasted his own blood as he grated his teeth back and forth in anger.

Velenka continued, "They found a remnant of Razor Shiver and a few others. If you surrender, it'll go much easier for you."

"Velenka," Gray gasped. "Are you crazy? The emperor is insane. How do you know he won't make me eat Barkley's head to prove I'm loyal?" The mako didn't answer. It was then that Gray understood. "You don't know what he's capable of, do you?"

"I took an awful chance coming here. This is a huge favour I'm doing for you!" She went on, either not noticing or not caring about the look of horror on his face. "You can't save everyone, Gray. If you throw yourself on the emperor's mercy, things may work out."

He shook his head in disbelief. "That's not a chance I'm willing to take, Velenka."

"Then everyone you know and care about is doomed!"

Gray backed out of the cramped cavern, not wanting to turn his back on the mako. If this was her idea of a favour, who knew what she might do if she had a chance to bite his tail?

"They won't be able to hide forever!" Velenka said, her eyes blazing with a weird intensity.

Gray slid out of the cavern – and found ten tattooed Indi Shiver sharkkind waiting. His heart sank. He was able to spot Trank in the pile of rocks by the door. "I thought you guaranteed my safety. I thought we had a deal!"

Trank fluttered off the sandy bottom, turning so he could look Gray in the eyes. "Sorry, pup. He offered a better deal. One where we keep breathing." The stonefish pointed a stubby fin into the distance, where Finnivus himself hovered!

The intricately tattooed tiger shark wore a dismissive smirk and had a cruel glint in his eye. He was carried on the back of a blue whale that hovered behind a wall of armoured guards. Seemingly on their own, Gray's fins and tail churned furiously as he stared at the haughty emperor. But his insides were chilled. Gray knew he could never allow this shark to decide the fate of his mother or any of his friends.

"So this is the sharkkind you spoke of?" said Finnivus. "We are not impressed."

"What's the matter with you?" Gray shouted at Finnivus. He looked over at the guards and their commander, the older shark they called the mariner prime. "And you! How can you allow him to order you to do such evil? Do you have any conscience at all?"

Finnivus's eyes blazed at Gray. "No one *allows* me to do anything! I – *we* – are the emperor of all the seven seas! None may disobey!"

Gray bristled, chopping his fins through the water. "All I see is a spoiled bully! But you won't get away with it! The good fins in the Big Blue will swim against you, you – chowderheaded flipper!"

There was an audible gasp from some of the guards. Finnivus's eyes went red, and he thrashed his tail around. "Did you just call me a chowderheaded flipper?" The emperor was maniacally angry now. "No one calls me names!" he yelled. "NO ONE!" He pointed at Gray with a trembling fin. "I – *we* want your head for dinner!"

"It didn't have to be this way," the mako told Gray sadly.

"And it's not going to be!" Gray roared, rocketing forward and catching the Indi mariners by surprise. He rammed the nearest one in the liver and ricocheted off two others.

"Seize him!" their commander shouted.

For all Gray's complaining, Takiza's training had transformed him. He was too quick for the armoured guards. Other armada mariners tried to catch him. Some clenched glinting ropes in their mouths – *chains* was the landshark word that flashed through Gray's mind. He knew he couldn't let the Indi sharks entangle him with those!

He accelerated towards Finnivus, cutting a hard turn that made his side hurt. The *squaline* adjusted their positions to block. Even wearing their metal coverings, they were so fast! But Gray wanted them to do that. This way he could go underneath the blue whale that Finnivus was riding. He finned it mercilessly in its soft underbelly.

The shock caused the whale to reflexively throw the emperor off his back and into the open waters. For any ordinary shark, this wouldn't have been a big deal, but Finnivus was no ordinary shark.

"Whalem! What's happening?" Finnivus yelled to his mariner prime, his voice cracking. Things weren't going as planned and now he was scared. Well, too bad! If things went smoothly, Gray would be eaten!

Whalem ordered, "Protect the emperor at all cost! Close ranks!"

Every armada mariner and *squaline* surrounded Finnivus immediately, which was *exactly* what Onyx had told Gray would happen.

Then members of the octopus clan, whom Gray and Barkley knew from the Coral Shiver, going all the way back to the bucket incident (and more importantly, who didn't work for Trank) rose from their hiding places on the ocean floor and squirted their black ink into the water.

Barkley had arranged for a meeting with the octos through Prime Minister Shocks while they were at Coral Shiver, and they were only too happy to help. Their ink blotted out the light from the random lumos in the area and put a putrid taste into the water. Now no one could follow him by sight or scent. Gray was going to owe them a huge thank you and a lot of fish, even though the older octos insisted on naming the plan *Operation Buckethead*. Dumb octos ...

Gray heard Whalem shout, "Fall back! Fall back!"

Finnivus shrieked even louder, "NO! WE DO NOT RETREAT! FIND HIM! I – *WE* ORDER IT!"

Yet Gray was already swimming into the thick greenie. He had escaped, but at what price to everyone he cared about?

CHAPTER 20

TYDAL WAS AFRAID TO TWITCH A FIN.
Doing so might draw unwanted attention from the
emperor, who hadn't stopped raging since he returned to
his newly conquered homewaters. Usually, Tydal went
with Finnivus on his swims outside the royal court in order
to serve him. However, when Finnivus travelled outside
the Indi Shiver homewaters, his wants and needs were
under *squaline* authority, so Tydal had been dismissed by
Finnivus and told to stay and "make this sad little place
more befitting for an emperor!" That had turned out to be
a very good thing.

The emperor's party was gone for only a little while.
During that time, Tydal had ordered the colourful crabs
and starfish forming their pleasing patterns to move
and create other hopefully *more* pleasing patterns. But
Finnivus returned too soon! The dwellers weren't nearly
finished, and Tydal couldn't give them instructions now.

They were moving slowly – which was how all crabs and starfish moved, by the way – into the shapes he'd told them to form and, to Tydal's ears, were making too much noise! Finnivus hadn't noticed yet, so great was his anger.

"WHO IS THIS SHARK NAMED GRAY?" the emperor yelled. "Why wasn't he captured?"

None of the younglings from the Line spoke. Even Finnivus's new favourite shark, Velenka, didn't dare say anything right now. Tydal had no idea who this *Gray* was, but he did know that the hunting party was supposed to capture him. Apparently, they hadn't. Finnivus hated it when *anything* didn't turn out exactly the way he wanted. He just wasn't used to that.

The clicking and clacking racket made by the moving crabs and starfish was *deafening*! It would only take a moment of silence for Finnivus to hear it and be displeased. Tydal's insides rumbled, and sharp pains jolted him as if his stomach were being bitten from the inside. Perhaps the shrimp and crab here didn't agree with him.

"I've been betrayed!" Finnivus huffed. Then he caught his mistake and said, "I mean, *we've* been betrayed!"

Tydal was sure he was hearing things when a voice said, "Your Majesty, no one betrayed you."

But it was real! Someone had dared to speak!

Everyone looked towards the offending fin who had interrupted the emperor's royal tantrum.

Of course, it was Whalem.

The fool was going to get himself killed! Everything went dead silent. Even the crabs and starfish had the good sense to stop moving. Finnivus looked across the court from his position atop a blue whale hovering over Riptide Shiver's conquered Speakers Rock. It was built up with bright yellow and orange starfish the way he liked, and the terraced greenie behind Finnivus framed him impressively. That fact was unimportant now, though. The emperor's mouth hung open.

Finally he asked, "What?"

Whalem sighed. Tydal could see that Whalem was going to make the horrible mistake of speaking his mind, or worse – *explaining* why Finnivus was *wrong*!

Before Tydal knew what he was doing – for he definitely would *not* have dared say a word if he had been thinking correctly – he blurted, "Dinner is ready, Magnificence!"

Now everyone in the royal court looked at Tydal. No one could believe he had spoken, including a very surprised Whalem. The rebuke was swift and immediate, though. Finnivus roared, "Mention dinner again, and *you'll* be the main course! DO YOU UNDERSTAND?"

Tydal thrust his face down until he was grovelling in the mud like the muck-sucker most of the court thought him to be. Thankfully, Finnivus turned his attention back to his mariner prime.

"What did you say?" the emperor asked. Even

though Finnivus spoke in a whisper, everyone around the court could clearly hear him. If Whalem would only grovel a little, maybe the situation could be saved. But Whalem wasn't like Tydal. The tiger was first in the Line of Indi Shiver, mariner prime, and commander of the armada. He *never* grovelled. Maybe that's why Tydal admired him.

"No one betrayed you, Finnivus. We were caught by surprise."

The beautiful mako took this as an attack and hissed, "I said, 'Be prepared'! I told you Gray was powerful and fast!"

A young spinner shark from the Line joined the fray – but carefully. "I remember Velenka saying this shark-kind was dangerous, but she didn't really make it clear just *how* dangerous. And Whalem, why didn't you take better precautions?"

It wasn't Whalem's fault, thought Tydal as he pressed his snout deeper in the mud. He'd overheard this part of the discussion before the group had left. Whalem had wanted to take a full battle fin, a hundred sharkkind, but Finnivus wouldn't hear of it. The emperor proclaimed that no one could stand against even a single Indi Shiver mariner. Then Whalem convinced Finnivus that it would be much more regal to have a cohort of *squaline* around himself to show off his greatness as well as a few dozen mariners. It was, all in all, a very skilful way of bending the emperor's will to his own. Their lack of proper guard was actually Finnivus's fault, but no one would be foolhardy enough to bring that up.

No one except Whalem, apparently. "I wanted to bring along a battle fin," the old tiger reminded the emperor, speaking to him as if he were an errant school fish!

"So you're saying I – WE – made a mistake?"

"How dare you, Whalem?" sputtered another pup from the Line. "How dare you accuse the emperor of such a thing?"

Whalem turned to the pup. "Shut your cod hole before I rip off your tail and feed it to you." Then he looked back at the emperor.

"Your Majesty," Whalem began. He looked tired to Tydal. "We are currently many leagues from our own Indi Ocean. We're not in our homewaters and do not know the territory. One large and fast shark-kind surprised us. When that happens it is our duty – my duty – to make sure you are protected first and foremost."

Whalem had totally ignored the emperor's question! That, in and of itself, was a grave crime. However, here was a chance for Finnivus to swim right by this whole ugly scene – if he would only take it, everything could go back to normal!

But the wicked young pups of the Line would never let an opportunity like this wriggle away from them.

One insisted, "Answer the emperor's question, Whalem! Are you saying he made a mistake?"

"Yes, answer the question!" added another.

Whalem gave the pups a look that might have killed two lesser sharks where they hovered. "No battle plans survive first contact –"

The emperor laughed in his tittering high-pitched way. "Are you saying this was a battle? One shark?"

"It turned into a battle, Finnivus."

"STOP CALLING ME FINNIVUS! I am the emperor! Emperor of the entire Big Blue! You are nothing but an old, krillfaced, jelly-brained drifter that my father should have got rid of a long time ago!"

Whalem's fins trembled, his rage barely under control. For a moment, he said nothing, but then he erupted, "Your father would be ashamed of you! You act like a spoiled pup! YOU'RE A DISGRACE!"

There was absolute silence.

The word *disgrace* seemed to echo through the waters of the court. No one dared move or even breathe. Tydal expected Whalem to be sent to the Sparkle Blue on the spot.

But Finnivus didn't rage. He seemed relieved. Tydal guessed it was because the emperor could finally get rid of Whalem. Regardless of the reason, Finnivus didn't yell.

"You are no longer my first, Whalem. I remove you from my Line. I strip you of command of the armada, as well as the title of mariner prime. You are nothing to me now." Finnivus settled on to Speakers Rock and ordered the commander of the *squaline*, "Take him into custody, but do not harm him. *We* will decide when royal justice shall be served."

AUZY-AUZY SHIVER

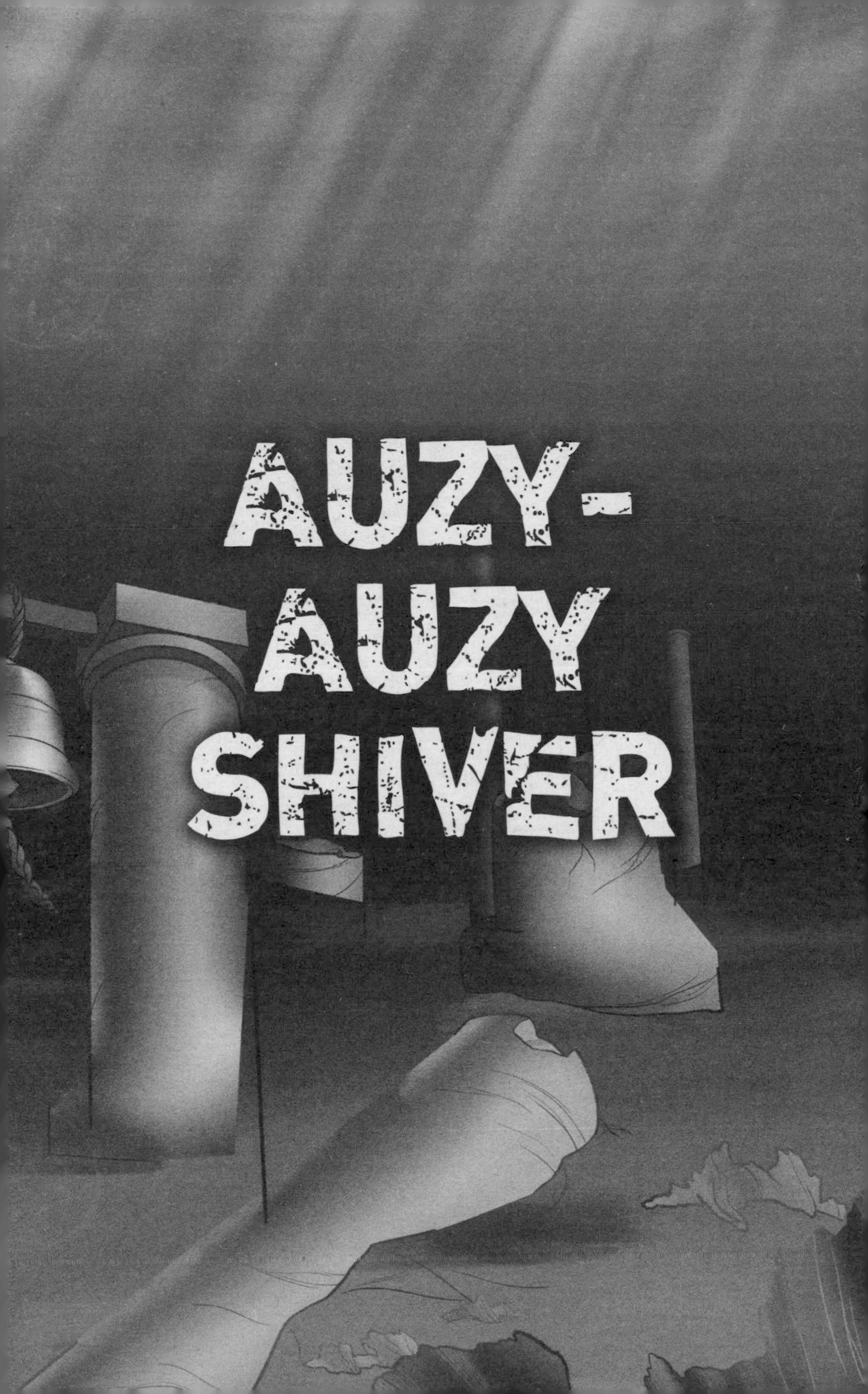

CHAPTER 21

"I TOLD YOU IT WAS A TRAP AND STILL YOU WENT,"
Takiza huffed.

"For the tenth time – I'm sorry!" Gray said, raising
his voice because he had to, not because he was being
disrespectful. They were heading down into the deep
open ocean, and it was hard to speak unless you yelled.
The words seemed to get sucked back into Gray's throat
unless he really spoke up. The fact that they were swimming away from Coral Shiver and his friends didn't help
his mood.

After a few hard days of exercises and drills, Gray
and Takiza swam past the Maw and towards the Atlantis Spine. To Gray's surprise, they didn't stop there but
headed up and over the towering undersea mountains of
the Spine. The mountains forming the Spine were awe-
inspiring. Their majestic greenie-covered crags contained
caverns that a fin could get lost in for days. Once over the

mountain range, the two swam down, down, down. They were deeper than the training grounds, in an area Takiza called the Azores.

"You should strive to keep your mouth closed and listen, Nulo! It is the only way you will learn." Takiza turned to see if he would say anything. Gray was so tired he couldn't muster the effort. They had been swimming for days. Was it days? He couldn't tell. There was very little light in the depths so near the Dark Blue.

"Your indescribably bad judgement has forced us on this journey sooner than I would have liked. Sooner than you are ready. See how you gasp and struggle? This could have been avoided – had you not angered the pup emperor."

Gray mumbled, "Sorry!" once more, but the ocean depths pressed the word back into his throat.

The frilly fish continued thinking out loud to himself. "Perhaps it's time. Perhaps your bumbling foolishness is, in a way, the current of destiny moving us. Who knows? Sometimes we are carried where the water wills, no matter our wishes."

"Okay, that sounded very important," Gray said with an effort. "Can you tell me what it means?" He sounded silly shouting when the gauzy-finned betta swam just a tail length in front of him.

Takiza looked at him crossly. "Everything I say is important, Nulo, or I wouldn't bother saying it. Watch and listen. Only then can you learn."

Gray struggled as they crested the top of the mountain range. He had to swallow several times before he could ask, "*What* is that?"

"That is the Atlantean capital, which the humans who lived there before it was sunk called Poseidous." Takiza dipped low into one of the evenly spaced valleys. These valleys weren't like the craggy areas between hills or mountains. *These* were perfectly smooth. While they were made of rock – Gray checked by slapping a tail against the one they were swimming through – the valleys were slippery to the touch. The channels *cut* into these rocks – or had the rocks been piled up to form the channels? – caught the current perfectly and made it very easy to swim. Greenie and coral had grown everywhere, but Gray could see humans – *giant* humans – between squarish caves that might be living spaces. The large guardians stood perfectly still as if waiting for unwary prey to swim close.

At the centre of the landshark homewaters, there was one immense human guiding six rearing animals, which seemed like the landshark versions of sea horses, with legs instead of fins and tails. The human held a gigantic weapon. It was much scarier than a spine shooter and had three massive prongs, each ending in barbs like the hooks he had seen humans use to catch fish. But how could the human stand so still? And how could it breathe underwater? Gray was sure landsharks couldn't stay underwater very long without cans of air on their backs.

Takiza saw him staring and chuckled. "It's a statue. A stone carving." He pointed with his fin to another group of these statues. "Humans liked chipping images of themselves into rock in the old days."

"Humans were much bigger in the old days!"

Takiza laughed. "No, they made the statues bigger to scare other landsharks away."

Gray looked around at a landshark version of Speakers Rock. It was a shallow bowl with rows of ridges rising upwards. The ridges were covered with greenie too, but Gray could tell there was the same type of smooth rock underneath. "How come no one ever mentioned this? I don't think Goblin knew, even though he told me stories about the Atlanteans."

"It's difficult for most sharkkind to swim this deep," Takiza told him. "It took weeks to train you, didn't it?"

Gray nodded. The landshark city was so fantastic, he had forgotten his difficulty breathing. It was hard to imagine that the same humans who flailed around in the ocean and had to use nets to catch their meals could build something like this. The humans Gray knew were dumb, fouling the very waters they fed from, but had to be respected because they were also extremely dangerous. "So why are we here?" he asked.

"Again you question me?" Takiza shook his head. He muttered to himself as he circled a thick strand of greenie and then smacked it with his fin. Gray then saw it wasn't a strand of greenie, but a landshark rope. It hit the metal surrounding it, which was in the shape of a jellyfish, and made a *BONNNNNNGGGGGGGGGG* sound that vibrated through the water in all directions.

Gray badly wanted to ask what that strange noise-making device was but had an answer soon enough when other sharks swam into view. He remembered that the object was called a *bell*. Landsharks used it to call others or warn of danger, but sharkkind could also hear its vibrations. Many came over, including a massive great white, almost as large as Gray, who was a golden colour.

Could it be? thought Gray.

The golden great white's booming voice cried out, "Takiza! What are you doing here so soon?"

The betta introduced the new shark. "He is why we are here. Gray, this is Lochlan Boola Naka Fiji, leader of the AuzyAuzy Shiver and the rightful king of the Sific."

"Lochlan . . ." Gray muttered with displeasure. So this was Takiza's favourite apprentice. Gray had to admit that the great white was impressive, especially with that striking colouring. He was a good metre larger than Striiker, which made him nearly half a metre bigger than Goblin used to be. Lochlan grinned in a friendly way, but Gray wasn't feeling very pleasant remembering all the times Takiza had mentioned this shark during training.

"What's the matter?" Lochlan asked, catching the sour look on Gray's face. "Did you eat a bad haddock? Stay away from the ones with yellowy eyes."

Gray shook his head. He shouldn't prejudge this

shark. "It's nothing. Nice to finally meet Takiza's favourite student."

"That will be enough speaking from you, Nulo," Takiza said.

Lochlan's eyes widened. He burst out laughing, waggling his fins up and down. "Is that what Takiza's been telling you? *I* was his favourite? Well, nice to finally do something right for once, eh?"

Takiza ruffled his own frilly fins in an odd way. Gray hadn't seen him do anything quite like it before. Then he understood the fleeting look on the betta's face. It was a touch of *embarrassment.*

"Wait a second," Gray began. "You weren't his prize student?"

This sent Lochlan into gales of laughter. "Prize student? He said I was his worst apprentice ever! He would always mention another finner named Ranier, who I absolutely *hated* after my first week! It was always, 'If only you could be more like Ranier, your training would be quicker' and 'Ranier never snapped even one coral spire,' things like that, over and over."

"Oh, *reeeeeeally,*" said Gray, giving Takiza a long look.

The little betta chopped his fins imperiously. "I only mentioned Lochlan to compare him at the *end* of his training badly – when I was finally able to teach him a few things – to you at the *beginning* of your training. Respectively, you two chowderheaded lumpfish are *tied* for being the *worst* apprentices I've ever had."

Both Gray and Lochlan laughed as Takiza ruffled his frilly fins again.

The massive great white nodded after catching his breath. "Gray, any friend of Takiza's is a friend of mine. And call me Loch."

"Okay, Loch," Gray answered. "Nice to meet you."

It was safe to say Gray liked Lochlan at once.

"Let me intro you to some of my Line. These are three of the fins I count on to tell me when I'm about to make a tail bender of a decision!"

"Which is often!" said a pretty whitetip reef shark. "My name is Kendra and I'm Loch's first."

Gray nodded and said hello, then found a smiling scalloped hammerhead grinning at him. "Xander del Hav'aii, call me Xander. I'm third."

Gray was slapped on the flank, hard. A small girl tiger shark said, "G'day! Name's Jaunt, and I'm fifth in Line of AuzyAuzy, which is kinda like being the smallest biter in the wet-wet. Sorry about not bringin' a prezzy, but we didn't know we wuz gonna yabber-jabber with you today."

Gray nodded nervously at Jaunt and then looked to the rest of the AuzyAuzy line, who seemed amused at his discomfort. "Umm, what language is she speaking? I understood about half."

"Too right!" yelled Lochlan as everyone laughed. "You got most of us beat, then! We hardly understand *anything* she says!"

Jaunt looked pained and flicked her tail. "Aww, come on! I'm no squiddily kelpie from the boonie-greenie! Maybe you guys should learn to speak proper like me!"

"Boonie-greenie!" Gray exclaimed. "I know that! But what's a squiddily kelpie?"

Everyone laughed again, even Jaunt this time. She slapped him on the flank and said, "*You're* a squiddily kelpie, ya big beauty!"

They spoke long into the night. Lochlan had lost his father and many friends when Finnivus had attacked. The golden great white grew sad telling the story. Lochlan's father had been a peace-loving ruler and was missed by everyone. The AuzyAuzy forces were currently scattered, but the rest were regrouping with Lochlan's second and fourth in Line until he was ready to lead them back to their homewaters. The journey had been delayed when Takiza asked him to come here.

Lochlan turned to Takiza. "So why bring this one sharkkind – what kind of shark are you, anyway?

"Umm –"

"He's a rare type of reef shark," Takiza told everyone. The betta had sworn Gray to secrecy about being a megalodon. He was to tell *no one* else.

"Good on ya," Jaunt said.

Now Kendra, the whitetip, spoke. "Gray seems like he could hold his own in a scuffle, for sure. But why just bring one fin to this fight?"

Now it was Takiza's turn to chuckle. "Oh, Gray is not

here to join you," he said. "I would like *you* to join *him* and repel Finnivus from the North Atlantis."

For a moment no one said a word.

Then Jaunt gave Gray another tail slap to the flank. "Good on ya, twice!"

CHAPTER 22

MARI WATCHED AS AN INDI SHIVER PATROL worked its way through the valley. It was her turn to guard the entrance and sound an alarm if the worst should happen and they were discovered by Indi Shiver. She was determined nothing like that would happen on her watch. Deep in the greenie field, a good hundred tail strokes past the Rock Lobster mound, something caught her attention. It took a while to make sure it wasn't just a fish – or her imagination.

It was Barkley. He slowly slid through the wide and thick blue and brown greenie stalks, almost crawling on the seabed like an octo. How he was able to move so stealthily was beyond her.

Barkley got under the entranceway to Coral Shiver, but he still didn't swim. It was a good thing he didn't. The Indi patrol had doubled back and would have seen him. The dogfish hovered, motionless, and was gently carried into the Coral Shiver homewaters by the mild current.

When he was safely underneath the canopy of greenie, Mari whispered, "You looked like you were dead, floating like that."

Barkley nodded. "And that's the point. If you stay in sync with the current, you're harder to spot. It's a sort of camouflage through movement."

Mari was impressed. Barkley was smart that way. He knew he wasn't the strongest shark in the Big Blue, so he'd learned to use anything he could to his advantage. Barkley could even follow Onyx without being seen by the cagey blacktip. Onyx was one of the best hunters she'd ever seen. Even though he was older and smaller than many shark-kind, he was almost always the first one to strike in a hunt.

She and Barkley reached the covered area of the Coral Shiver homewaters, and Onyx swam quietly to them. "How'd it go?" he asked Barkley. The dogfish shook his head. Onyx sighed. "Come on. He's going to want to hear it from you."

Onyx led Barkley and Mari to a more secluded area in the homewaters. Everyone was waiting there.

"How bad?" asked Quickeyes.

"We can't swim out of the area without being seen," Barkley told everyone. "Their patrols are thick, with no gap between them where we'd have the time to leave. And Indi varies their patrols, so there's no pattern. Or at least, none that I could figure out."

Striiker slapped Onyx's flank. "Then we fight our way out!" he whisper yelled.

In the past Barkley would have immediately put down the great white's idea. The dogfish wasn't usually diplomatic when he thought an idea was a bad one. Now he waited for someone else to do that. Striiker seemed to take having his ideas dismissed by Quickeyes, Sandy, Shell or even Snork, better than when Barkley did it. "There may be safer options," Sandy told Quickeyes. "Waiting for the perfect time would be better than getting caught while half of us are still inside."

That was true. The same thing that made the homewaters defensible also made it hard to leave all at once – a narrow choke point was the only exit. Mari shuddered to think what the mad Emperor Finnivus would do to those who were captured.

"Starving as we wait isn't a great option," Onyx groused. Striiker agreed, of course, nodding. "The few of us that do go outside can't bring home enough fish for everyone."

"It's only a matter of time before one of us makes a mistake and tips them off, isn't it?" Snork said fearfully. "I hope it's not me."

Shell patted the sawfish on his flank. "You're one of the fins who can hunt quietly. I know you won't do anything jelly-brained."

Snork seemed to gain strength from the bull's comment. For a shark who didn't say much, when Shell did speak, his words counted.

"We'll starve!" Striiker insisted. "Quickeyes, you have to lead!"

"And I am." Quickeyes flicked his angled thresher tail into the sand, causing a muddy cloud to rise. "But we have to figure out a way to move without being eaten. When I do, you'll be the first to know."

"But –" Striiker stopped speaking when Onyx shook his head.

"What youse needs is a distraction!" exclaimed a gruff voice.

Mari was able to find its source and wasn't surprised. There was only one fish she'd ever met with that accent: Trank. She whirled. "How dare you show your little krillface in here?"

"Ay, ay – no need for personal insults. I'm here to help."

"Like you *helped* Gray by betraying him?" Striiker said, batting the much smaller fish with his tail.

Trank recovered from the disturbance caused by the swipe and glared. "Youse got no idea of the pressure Gafin's under!"

"*He's* the one?" asked Sandy, her voice rising. "This, this – little –" Sandy had been told about the stonefish's betrayal of Gray. While Trank didn't seemed worried about any of the other sharks, he backed away from Gray's mother. Smart fish.

Quickeyes swam in front of her. "Please, Sandy, don't get near it. It's a stonefish."

"We should kill it," said Onyx. "Can't let it tell Indi where we are."

"Quit callin' me *it*, sharkkind! An' like I said, I'm here to help."

Quickeyes, as leader, was about to order the stonefish's death. Barkley saw this and interrupted before he could. "Wait. If Trank's here, they've already found us. Let him talk."

"Smart fin, youse are. Found you three days ago. Gafin was deciding what to do."

"Sell us out or come here with an offer?" asked Quickeyes.

Trank shrugged. "Somethin' like that. Gafin feels bad about double-crossin' Gray. But he wants youse to know that he knew about the deal youse set up with the Coral Shiver octo clan in case Gray was trapped at Slaggernacks by Velenka and Indi Shiver. There's nothing he don't know about dwellers in the Big Blue. And he let that happen – which *let* Gray escape."

Barkley looked to Mari for her opinion. For some reason, she liked it when he did this. "He seems to be telling the truth," she told him.

"Wonder of wonders," Striiker said in his cutting way, getting a stare from Trank.

Snork shook his toothy bill from side to side. "I still don't believe him."

"Look, Gafin doesn't like this Finnivus clown fish or his crew. He'd just as soon see 'em go back where they came from."

Several of the group laughed in disbelief. "Gee, us too. Are you going to battle their armada?"

Trank smiled, his little fins moving back and forth. "Fightin' snout to snout, that's not our style, see? But we can give youse a very nice edge."

"How helpful of you," said the amused Quickeyes. "But in case you hadn't noticed, we're stuck here, starving, and don't have an army to fight them."

"Moving day – that's in the future," Trank told everyone. "Like I said, youse needs to figure out a distraction. As far as food, I think youse all can lose a few pounds, but I come bearing gifts – you know, to make up for what happened to Gray."

Mari's mouth began watering before she knew what was happening. Then she saw it – a giant lobster crawling up the rocks near where they were meeting. In its claws were two fat hake fish! And behind that lobster was a giant crab with a couple more fish. And another, and another, forming a line of shellheads marching on the seabed – all bringing food!

"You know, my opinion is suddenly all turned around on Trank," Striiker said as he gulped down a tasty haddock. "Still don't totally trust you, though."

"And the beauty of it is you don't have to just yet," Trank replied.

Quickeyes gave the stonefish a stare and clicked his jaws shut a few times before saying anything. "Thank you for the fish. It won't be forgotten. But we wouldn't last a minute fighting Finnivus's armada."

Trank nodded. "You'd need an army. So you couldn't beat them today, but youse never know what tomorrow brings. Or tonight, for that matter."

The stonefish turned towards the blackness of the cliff that plunged almost to the Dark Blue. Rising from the dark was a massive hammerhead, followed by another fifty sharks.

It was when she saw the scars that Mari knew who it was and gasped.

"Ripper!"

CHAPTER 23

"AGAIN!" TAKIZA YELLED FROM HIS POSITION BY a large statue in the centre of the Atlantean stadium. This was the area that Gray had thought was the land-shark version of Speakers Rock. He'd been a bit mis-taken. Takiza told him that the large, bowl-like structure was for sports and training. This wide-space place was where landsharks would play games and others could watch. It also made a perfect practice range for Lochlan and Gray, who had grown accustomed to the depths of the Atlantean city of Poseidous. It was much easier for Gray to move and speak now.

Lochlan smiled wickedly, his golden hue noticeable even at these depths. "Would you like another shot at the title, mate?"

"Don't mind if I do," Gray answered, churning his tail and rushing the giant great white. He couldn't help but grin back. This was such fun! He was learning so much, even though he was beaten every time. It seemed Lochlan deserved every complimentary thing Takiza had ever said about him. If Gray could learn to be half as good as the great white, he'd be the best fighter in the North Atlantis.

He rocketed straight at Lochlan, performing Cuttle-fish Strikes, but was blocked when Lochlan countered the pectoral fin attack with Swordfish Parries. Gray feinted Sunfish Greets the Morn and seamlessly moved into the dorsal attack, Topside Rip. He was learning to proceed smoothly from one move into another, then another, rather than think of each as a single manoeuvre. When you strung the moves together this way, fighting was more like a dance.

Unfortunately, Lochlan wasn't fooled by the fake and was ready with a perfectly executed Orca Bears Down. He drove Gray into the seabed, causing a cloud of silt to muddy the cold water. If there were a way to beat Lochlan in single combat, Gray hadn't found it.

"Hold!" said Takiza. "I can take no more! My eyes are pained by your clumsy show. I have other matters to attend to so I will leave for a time. Keep training, for though you are both hopeless, I believe everyone you will fight against is even more pathetic than either of you." Takiza reminded them that they wouldn't have time to search for food once they entered the waters patrolled by Indi Shiver. Gray got the creeping feeling that the betta was involved in many different weighty things in the Big Blue. But if this fight wasn't important enough to spend all his time on, how much trouble was the watery world in? The thought made him feel like a tiny guppy.

Later, as Gray finished off the last of a large cod, he said, "I thought it was bad to fight on a full stomach."

"Never stuff yourself right before a battle," Lochlan told him. "That's true enough. But we'll be swimming hard for a good while, so we need to keep up our strength." He looked at his third and gave him a nudge. "What's the matter, Xander?"

Gray was still getting used to Xander's unusual appearance – unusual compared to what he thought of as a *normal* hammerhead. Hammerheads were one of the weirder-looking sharks in the Big Blue with their heads seemingly stuck on the wrong way. Being a scalloped hammerhead, Xander had indentations on his long forehead that made him look as if he were perpetually thinking about something. But in this case, he really was. For a moment, it seemed as though he didn't want to speak.

"You know, the Line only works if you tell Loch what your problem is," Kendra said.

"I don't think we should be doing this," Xander said after a moment. He turned to Gray and added, "Sorry. No disrespect to you or your cause."

Jaunt tail-slapped Xander on the flank. "Since when are you the sorta biter that swims away from a scrumble?"

"We're not ready for it," Xander replied. "I've gone

over this in my head a dozen times, and it always comes up the same. This is a bad call."

"How so?" asked Lochlan. The great white didn't get angry when challenged the way Goblin would have, or shout Xander down as Striiker most likely would have. And Finnivus would have undoubtedly done something horrible. But Lochlan actually wanted to know why his trusted friend thought his idea was bad.

So this is what a good king is like, Gray thought.

Xander continued, "We're not prepared to face off against Indi."

Jaunt became incensed. "They deserve what's coming!"

"I'm not saying that isn't true, Jaunt," Xander answered. "But having truth and goodness on our side is no replacement for a fully loaded armada of our own. The timing is bad." Loch had mentioned that most of their forces were hiding in the Sific, far away, with only fifty sharkkind here to protect him. The hammerhead now looked to Lochlan. "We need time to get ready. And we can only do that as long as Finnivus *doesn't* know we exist."

Lochlan remained silent for a moment. "You're right, Xander. But we can't just turn tail and allow Finnivus free rein to do evil. Sometimes a fin has to swim out and be counted."

"If Finnivus finds out you're alive, he'll scour the ocean for you! That mariner prime they have is no fool."

Then Xander whispered, "If the numbers are in his favour when we meet, he'll win."

Gray couldn't hover idly by any longer. "Excuse me," he began. "I really appreciate you considering helping me. But this is my fight, for my shiver and my family. I'll do the best I can with what I have. I don't want you to lose your chance of stopping Finnivus later. It might be the only real chance anyone has."

Lochlan bumped flanks with Gray. "Well said, that. But we can't allow the emperor to tighten his grip here. And we have the element of surprise. By giving him more to think about in the North Atlantis, he'll have fewer sharkkind available to control the Sific. That's good for when we make our move there." He looked at Xander. "I understand if you want to put your strength where you think it'll do the most good," Lochlan told him. "Go back to our fins in the Sific. Gather and train them."

The group waited for Xander's reply. Finally, the big hammerhead nodded. "Loch, I'd swim to the bottom of the Dark Blue and fight a prehistore monster for you. If you think this is the right move, I'm with you, flank to flank, mate."

Lochlan and Xander slapped fins.

"What are you flapping your large mouths about this time?" asked Takiza, who once again appeared out of nowhere. "You chatter like sea monkeys."

"It seems we've decided to help with Gray's fight!" Lochlan told him in a booming voice.

"It's always sensible to do what I tell you to do," Takiza responded without a hint of sarcasm.

Jaunt looked over at Gray. "Is he always like this?"

"Way worse!" he answered.

Takiza began giving orders. "Lochlan, take your sharkkind over near the Riptide Shiver homewaters and wait. Do not attack before I tell you to. I shall repeat myself, as I did countless times during your training: do not attack before I say so."

"Easier said than done," remarked Kendra.

"I know!" Takiza exclaimed. "She is the wisest fish among you! But I have some delicate plans in place, and if you rush in and attack like some foolish rumble fish, you'll ruin everything."

"Would you like to share the reason why?" Lochlan asked, amused.

Takiza sighed as if he really didn't want to reveal anything, but then relented. "We have to save someone from Finnivus who won't want to be saved."

Kendra released a frustrated stream of bubbles from her gills. "Do you know how annoying that is? When you say something like that and don't give any specifics?"

Takiza was amused by this. "Why, yes, I do!" He grinned. "The shark we need to save is named Whalem, and until a few days ago he was the mariner prime of Finnivus's armada."

"Finnivus stripped Whalem's rank? He won't like that. He's a proud finner," Xander said with wonder.

The AuzyAuzy Line were all familiar with the old tiger. "Maybe we do have a chance."

Takiza nodded. "I only hope trusting Barkley and Onyx to sneak inside Indi's royal court to free him wasn't a fatal mistake on my part. And theirs, I suppose."

If the betta wanted Gray's total attention, he had definitely succeeded. But the frilly fish wasn't finished. He turned to Gray and said, "Oh, and I need you to swim down into the Maw to get something for me."

CHAPTER 24

"STOP!" BARKLEY WHISPERED, JUST LOUD ENOUGH for the light current they crawled against to carry the warning to Onyx and no one else.

The blacktip settled on to the sandy bottom without stirring a grain of sand. For someone who didn't normally sneak around, Onyx was very good at it. Neither twitched a muscle as an Indi Shiver patrol circled round the craggy shelf marking the east boundary of the Riptide homewaters and passed above where he and Onyx hid, silent as sea wraiths.

Barkley resumed moving carefully forward through the greenie, barely a flipper length off the seabed. He shuddered to think what would happen if they were caught and dragged before Finnivus.

The dogfish had known at a young age that he could swim more quietly than most. It was natural that as the bullies around the reef had got bigger, he'd got better at remaining silent and safely hidden from them. Not everyone could do this. Striiker, for example, was terrible at stalking. He was a great hunter because of his strength and size, but he could sneak around as well as a human splashing about in the Big Blue.

Barkley signalled for Onyx to follow. When Barkley and Gray were little, they had always thought of Onyx as a humourless curmudgeon. The blacktip ordered shiver sharks this way and that. But they'd never realized that whenever Onyx *did* speak, those sharks listened because he was usually right. Now, if Barkley had to pick someone to help him when it was a matter of life and death, after Gray, he would choose Onyx.

He felt a nip at his tail. Barkley knew Onyx would only do that for a good reason, so he allowed his body to go limp, the tide carrying it slightly. The blacktip eased next to him. "Stay away from Speakers Rock. It's the royal court, so there'll be even more guards."

Barkley nodded. There was no need to answer with words, and it was dangerous to speak here. He adjusted his route accordingly. He and Onyx had formulated this plan after Takiza had come to them with his insane idea – steal the imprisoned mariner prime of the Indi armada from under the emperor's snout. "And what else would you like us to do tonight?" Barkley had grumbled to himself.

They hugged the weedy bottom of a coral reef which gave them some cover.

They weren't even going to lead Whalem to safety tonight. Onyx was sure that if they tried to take him without his permission, the mariner prime would raise an alarm. Because of honour and royal etiquette – *pfah!* – Whalem would have to be asked first: *nicely*. As if you really needed a reason *not* to want your head served on a platter! But Whalem's honour wouldn't allow him to betray the emperor, even if Finnivus were insane. They had to convince him. That meant Barkley and Onyx needed to get close enough to talk with Whalem without being noticed. Yikes!

Luckily, Barkley knew every centimetre of these homewaters from his time as a member of Goblin Shiver. How small the problems they'd struggled with then seemed now. The duelling between Goblin and Razor seemed as important as pups fighting after school compared with what everyone faced today.

Another bump from Onyx. Barkley looked back, and the blacktip gestured to the left. Ah! There it was. The prison. The structure itself looked like nothing Barkley had ever seen in the Big Blue. That's because it had been made by landsharks thousands of years ago. Onyx had told the story of how the prison was given to the first king of Indi Shiver by the Atlanteans. Barkley had no idea how they had got the thing here. Maybe a whale had carried it? Unlike most of the ancient landshark items Barkley had seen on the bottom of the ocean, this cage wasn't covered with barnacles and greenie. This object shone as if it were new.

The last eighteen metres were the hardest. The constant patrols forced them to stop many times, and all Barkley could do was shut his eyes and will himself to be invisible. Finally, they reached the cage. So stealthy was their approach that Whalem didn't sense a thing until Onyx spoke.

"Mariner Prime, please be quiet and listen," he said. To Whalem's credit, he didn't start or twitch a muscle. His eyes focused on Onyx and widened slightly. Onyx continued, "I see you still remember me after all these years."

"Get on with it," hissed Barkley. The mariner prime heard Barkley's voice but couldn't see where he was hiding in the thick greenie.

"I come under a term of truce and would like you to let me speak without rousing anyone. Is that acceptable?"

There was a slight nod from the ancient tiger shark.

"Takiza asks, if we can free you, would you come with us? But not only that, he asks that you help us defeat the emperor."

After a moment, Barkley saw an almost imperceptible shake of the old tiger's head.

Onyx didn't bother asking again, saying only, "Thank you for your time, sir." He bobbed his head and motioned for them to leave the way they came in.

Barkley was incensed. They had come too far at too much risk to turn back with nothing. Onyx saw his anger and started to say, "Indi Shiver is very different –" but Barkley swam past and took his spot. "What are you doing? Get back here!" the blacktip urged.

Barkley shook his head. He would have his say. The mariner prime watched in silence as Barkley waited for a group of richly tattooed mariners from the armada to swim lazily past, followed by two armoured *squaline*.

"If you want to lie down on the emperor's platter, that's your choice," Barkley hissed. "But not coming with us because you think you owe crazy Finnivus your loyalty isn't honourable – it's cowardly."

Whalem's eyes blazed, but Barkley wasn't going to leave without saying everything on his mind. "You owe that flipper nothing except a good tail slap to the face. You owe it to me and everyone else in the Big Blue to help stop him – which probably isn't possible, anyway. So your honour can be served, along with our seasoned heads, when we lose."

Whalem whispered, "Who are you to talk to me this way, pup?"

"I'm Barkley. And no matter what you think, it isn't honourable to take the easy way out and leave us with this giant mess that you're at least partially responsible for! So once more, if we can get you out – which we probably can't – will you help us stop Finnivus?"

Barkley's throat was sore from speaking so quietly, yet with such hissing force. He couldn't believe that no one had seen or heard anything, and he gratefully edged back into the greenie next to Onyx. The mariner prime seemed unmoved. If he was insulted, well, that was too bad. "Okay, *now* we can go," Barkley told the astonished blacktip.

It was then Onyx nudged Barkley, gesturing with a fin at the Indi armada commander.

Whalem was *grinning*.

He whispered, "All right. If you can get me out, I'll help you."

INTO THE DARK BLUE

CHAPTER 25

GRAY LOOKED DOWN FROM THE SHARP LEDGE into the blackness of the Maw. The pressure at these depths gave him an uncomfortable, queasy feeling. But the yawning chasm of the Maw scared Gray to his very core.

He was wearing the greenie torture harness from his practice session. The rock was in the harness, but at least right now it lay on the seabed as Gray hovered near the sand. Apparently, the rock's weight would help him swim to the bottom of the Dark Blue.

Takiza had trained him for this very task. Gray got chills thinking about it. Whether those chills were about swimming down into the Maw or about Takiza having planned for this day, Gray didn't know. He felt ashamed that Lochlan and the sharks from AuzyAuzy Shiver were swimming to protect his family and friends without him. In a way, Gray envied them. Waiting on the edge of the abyss, he discovered that he would rather face the entire Indi armada than swim down into the depths of the Dark Blue.

"Shiro, I'd feel much more comfortable –"

Takiza cut Gray off. "Yes, you'd feel much more comfortable if I came with you. Perhaps I can stroke your flanks and recite a story on the way?"

"Yech!" Gray shuddered. "That image is nasty. I was going to ask if I could take the harness off for a little while. But if you do know where this glowing greenie is . . . and since you're better than I am in every way –"

"Of course, I am! Stop talking foolishness, Nulo. If I could do this, I would. But you must, and you need to succeed! Do you understand? This is the most important thing you've done in your short, pampered life! So far, anyway."

Gray nodded as if he understood the weight of the matter, but he didn't really. Takiza was such an amazing fish. There was no way that Gray could do the incredible things the little betta could. It seemed as if Takiza were sending Gray to his death. And the fact that Takiza kept saying, "I am sorry I may be sending you to your death," didn't help the situation at all.

"Again, you only have to say that once," Gray replied when Takiza repeated it again. "I'm not going to forget."

"Then tell me again what you will do when you arrive at the seabed below," ordered the betta.

Even though it was at least the fifteenth time Gray

had repeated the instructions, he got right to it. "I will descend to the bottom of the Dark Blue –" Gray quickly corrected himself: "The bottom of this particular area of the ocean and find the glowing green kelp called mared-soo, the energy plant. When I'm there, I exchange the rock for greenie and swim back to you."

Takiza grew cross and snapped his fins out. "Don't *exchange* anything. Load the greenie – but don't eat any – into the harness *before* you remove the rock. Your body will not remain at the bottom without the rock. So it's important to do it in the proper order – greenie first, *then* remove the stone. Remember, Nulo!"

"I will!" Gray shouted. "What are we waiting for? If you're not coming and time is so short, shouldn't I get going?"

Gray could see Takiza was about to explode but didn't care. He'd never felt so scared in his life – not even at Tuna Run facing off against Goblin. Here, waiting by the ever-black waters of the Maw, he felt cold and terrified. It was just too much!

But before Takiza could yell at him, a prehistore *horror* raised itself from the gloom below. It was nearly circular and had skin that was at once black, slimy *and* pasty. Though it was tiny compared with Gray, it was three times Takiza's size and almost entirely composed of a giant mouth stuffed with bristling teeth. The razor-sharp needle teeth were so big, it was hard to see how the little monster could close its mouth without wounding itself. Gray tried to swim away but was stuck fast because of the rock inside his harness.

"Look out!" Gray shouted. "Behind you!"

Takiza turned, unconcerned. "Finally!" he snorted. "Have you no concept of time?"

"Ah, no actually," said the prehistore fish. "Kind of dark where we live."

"*You know this thing*?" Gray asked.

Someone said, "Hey! You'd better mind your mouth, or else I'm going to come over there and teach you a lesson!" But the prehistore fish's lips didn't move. In fact, this was a completely different voice. Then Gray saw there was a much tinier dweller, an even uglier fish stuck like a barnacle on the first horrible-looking fish's side. In fact, the smaller ugly fish seemed to be *feeding* on the larger one with its *fangs*.

"Oh, oh! Gross!" Gray pointed with his fin. "You have a nasty on your side! A sea tick or something! You should definitely go to a doctor fish and get that removed!"

The larger horrific-looking fish seemed put off and cocked its head to the side as it addressed Takiza. "Digging in the shallow end of the kelp bed for your apprentices these days?"

"Sadly, this is the age we live in," Takiza said, shaking his head.

"Sea tick? Did that chowderhead just call me a sea tick?" asked the smaller fish indignantly.

"Calm down, honey," said the larger ugly fish.

Finally Takiza made some introductions. "This is Briny and her husband, Hank, and I'll thank you to be respectful of them!" the betta said to Gray. "They are humpback anglerfish –"

"Devilfish!" yelled Hank, the small one.

Takiza looked at Briny curiously as Hank's face returned to press into her side, sucking blood like a leech. "I was under the impression it was rude to call you that."

"It was." Briny seemed embarrassed. "But we changed our minds. We ladies don't like talking about our humps."

"Besides, devilfish sounds way cooler!" Hank added.

With that, Takiza turned to Gray and continued, "These *devilfish* live in the depths that you fear to swim. They will lead you to the maredsoo."

Gray felt awful. "I'm sorry," he said to the pair. "I – I'm not from around here."

"We figured that out, jelly-brain!" said Hank.

Takiza shook his head in disapproval. "There is no need to race and prove yourself a bumpkin when meeting someone. They will find out soon enough. Now, lift the stone and follow them!"

"Yes, Shiro," Gray said, feeling like a total loser. With a heave and an upwards thrust, the rock slowly rose from the seabed. "Thank you for not making me go alone."

"Are you speaking again?" Takiza asked Gray. "Lift and swim!"

"He is a strong one," said Briny. "I'll give him that."

"That would explain the lack of brains," Hank told her. "All the big fish are dummies."

Gray looked at Takiza, who just grinned. "Oh, so you agree?"

"Come on, pup! We have a party to get to after this!" said Hank. He flapped his fins in annoyance but didn't remove his fangs from Briny's slimy side.

Gray looked down at the Maw's chasm. It was dark and terrifying. Gray shuddered, gave the wan sunlight coming from above one last look, and let the weight of the rock pull him down into the blackness.

As he was swallowed by the Dark Blue, Takiza yelled after him. "Make sure to come back, Nulo! Your training is not complete and you gave me your word!"

Gray gulped. He should have said something back, but the darkness had his total attention. Soon the pressure was squeezing him even more. The large rock nestled inside his harness pulled him down, down, down, so the water whooshed past his ears. It grew colder as it got darker. Chills, from the cold and Gray's anxiety, marched down his spine and settled in the pit of his stomach.

"You doing okay?" asked Hank after a time. "You look a little peaky."

Gray wanted to throw up. A fish the colour of black slime was telling him he looked unwell. And he probably did after . . . how long had they been descending? An hour? A day? He couldn't tell in this black vastness.

"Gray?" called out Briny. For the first part of the trip, Briny had held on to the harness with her teeth. Now she could easily swim by his side as the rock was pulling Gray more slowly. His teeth were chattering, so he couldn't answer right away. "Gray, can you hear me? Can I ask you a question?"

"Oh-oh, s-s-sure," he stuttered. The pressure from the depths was making his head swim. Were they still going down?

"Don't ask him," said Hank. "You always do this. Makes everyone uncomfortable."

"It does not," Briny answered.

"Least put your light on, so he can see you."

"Oh, you're right! Where are my manners?" A little light brightened and dangled in front of Briny's jagged rows of teeth. It took a conscious effort not to swim towards the light in this darkness. Gray realized it would be very helpful for hunting in this black place.

In the light Gray could see Briny look at him self-consciously – if a fish who looked like a prehistore nightmare could seem self-conscious – before screwing up her courage. "Does my husband make my hump look fat?"

Gray caught a look of panic from Hank before saying through chattering teeth, "N-no, B-b-b-briny. I think Hank looks sl-slimming on you."

Briny became very pleased.

Hank gave Gray a fins-up and said, "Hey, you're

okay! And you'll be glad to know we're nearly halfway there already!"

"We're making very good time," said Briny matter-of-factly.

Gray's heart began thudding in terror as if it would burst out from his chest entirely. They weren't even *halfway* there yet?

CHAPTER 26

THE ROYAL COURT WAS ALL IN A BUSTLE. Velenka had heard that an intruder had been captured just off the western edge of the heavily patrolled Riptide homewaters. She watched Finnivus stare imperiously from his place, high above everyone on one of his blue whales. Framed by the terraced greenie behind him, the young tiger shark looked royal indeed.

Then Velenka suddenly spotted the prisoner. The battle-scarred hammerhead could be no one else.

Ripper!

So he hadn't been killed by the armada's advance guard as she had thought. The *squaline* had secured Ripper by looping an ancient chain through his mouth. The ends were attached to two other armoured hammerheads, so Ripper couldn't make a rush at the emperor. There was also a device in his mouth that prevented him from biting down all the way. The massive hammerhead didn't struggle, allowing himself to be led down the main aisle to the foot of Finnivus's well-guarded throne. It seemed odd for a sharkkind as proud and strong as Ripper to come so easily.

"What have we here?" asked Finnivus.

"Your Magnificence," Tydal announced, "a prisoner caught by your armada mariners."

Finnivus glared at his first court shark. "Obviously, Tydal. Now tell us something we don't know."

The brown-and-yellow epaulette shark bobbed his head. "Apologies. This hammerhead, who calls himself Ripper, says he was the first in the Line for Riptide Shiver."

"Really?" Finnivus mused, looking over at Velenka. "I thought we ate those flippers."

"Ripper was Goblin's first," Velenka explained. "But Goblin left when your mighty armada arrived. I thought Ripper also turned tail and swam away." There was a bloom of anger in the hammerhead's eyes at Velenka's words, and she was glad he was bound and chained.

"Well?" Finnivus asked Ripper. "Is that true? Are you a coward?"

The device in his mouth made it difficult to speak, but not impossible. Clearly whoever had made it had given some thought to this very situation. "Lies," the hammerhead spit. "And Goblin didn't leave. She killed him."

A murmur rose within the court. "I did no such

thing!" yelled Velenka, voice rising. "I worshipped my leader despite his bad decisions. But he would have swum the Sparkle Blue, anyway, because Emperor Finnivus Victor Triumphant – the rightful ruler of all the Big Blue – was coming."

Finnivus laughed his tittering laugh. "That's true, we suppose. Should we eat him and be done with it? From the looks of him, he won't be tasty no matter what the royal seasoners do."

This would solve all of Velenka's problems so she immediately agreed: "Yes, excellent idea!"

"Oh, I could give you some great advice," Ripper told everyone. The court let out a gasp. Apparently, they weren't used to anyone, especially a prisoner, talking so directly to their ruler.

Finnivus's eyes blazed. He certainly felt insulted. "And what would that be?"

"Two things. First, Coral Shiver has formed a treaty with an old friend of yours, King Lochlan Boola something-or-other and his AuzyAuzy Shiver. They're gathering their forces about a day's swim from the east side of these homewaters."

"WHAAAT?" shouted Finnivus. "Impossible! I destroyed them! I destroyed *him*! That can't be true! Commander, is it true?"

The new spinner commander who had been promoted to Whalem's position was caught by surprise. "I – I – there's no sign of that from the patrols."

"YOU'RE NOT SURE? You're not sure that Lochlan isn't here with an armada! He hates me, that one! I had to strike first! But that's beside the point! The point is YOU'RE NOT SURE!"

"I am! The prisoner is lying. We haven't seen anything."

Ripper was unconcerned. "You wouldn't. They're hidden, call themselves the Golden Rush. He's coming for you." The hammerhead smiled maliciously.

Finnivus swished his tail furiously. "Take an entire battle fin and find them! But do not attack. I want to be present for my victory. And their destruction."

"Yes, Magnificence!" yelled the new commander before swimming off as fast as he could.

The emperor looked back at Ripper. "You said there were two things. What's the second? Speak. I command it."

"The second is . . . watch your tail, pal." Ripper gestured towards Velenka. The court let out another louder gasp. "If you're going to let this one near you, you'd better watch it closely."

Velenka couldn't help herself. "Kill him!" she yelped as everyone was shouting and talking at once. "He's insulting you!"

The emperor whirled. "I give the orders around here, Velenka! You do what *we* say, and *we* say . . . shut your cod hole!"

Velenka went silent and said nothing more. Unfortunately, she should have spoken up earlier. She should have listened to that nagging feeling she'd had when they had brought in Ripper without a struggle. If Velenka had thought about it more, she would have realized that the scarred hammerhead would *never* allow himself to be brought in without a fight.

Amid all the shouting and accusations, what Velenka, Finnivus, the *squaline* and everyone else in court failed to notice was one sneaky little dogfish swimming unseen, right past their distracted snouts.

CHAPTER 27

DOWN, DOWN, DOWN, THEY WENT INTO THE blackness of the Maw. Gray's mind boggled. How could there be so much ocean? The world he swam in was just a tiny drop of water compared to the immense area below.

But who lived down here? What exactly was he passing?

Perhaps it was better to slide downwards not knowing. The glimpses Gray saw were unsettling. At one point, there were a thousand tiny lights floating in the darkness, just like the stars in the sky. It was only when Gray got close that he realized that every single one of these lights belonged to a devilfish, or to their larger cousin, the deep-sea angler. That fish was like a puffer squashed flat with a wedge taken out for the mouth. In place of the missing wedge were bristling needle teeth jutting in all directions.

Gray caught glimpses of other horrors that didn't give themselves away with lumo lures. Briny and Hank pointed out the eerie black chimera, the mantis shrimp with its deadly claws and the deep sea swallower – that could eat a fish three times its own size in one gulp! And there were deadly jellyfish, giant squid and even bigger octos that dwarfed Gray as they spread their arms to embrace their lightless kingdom.

"Are-are we th-th-there yet?" Gray asked, shivering from the intense cold and pressure.

"We'll get there when we get there!" Hank grumbled. "One more word and we'll turn around!"

Gradually, Gray had to work to swim downwards. The water became lighter than he was, even with the rock's added weight, something Takiza had warned him would happen. He was stiff and sore from the vicious cold that froze him inside and out. Gray panted as he fought the elements, swimming his way down, down, down.

"There it is!" said Briny as she scooted in front of Gray. The devilfish was a poor swimmer in the waters Gray called home but did just fine here. Briny shone her glowing lure and illuminated the area where the ghostly, glowing maredsoo grew. There was no other greenie or coral here. This one plant grew by itself in the desolate sand and stood alone as if waiting for Gray.

He wanted nothing more than to get the magical

greenie and head up to Takiza. Exhausted beyond belief, he tilted himself to get rid of the rock inside the harness – only to hear Hank yell, "No, no, no!"

It was then Gray remembered: get the maredsoo first, then lose the rock. But it was too late. The stone rolled out and Gray shot upwards as if he were being pulled by his tail! He was no longer heavy enough to stay at this depth!

Hank looked at Briny and said, "See? The big ones never think."

Frantically, Gray shook off his numbing terror of the blackness and cold, focusing on the glowing plant. He panted, pumping the thick water through his gills, furiously swimming for the bottom. For all his exhausting efforts, Gray only inched closer with agonizing slowness. The tail length he was short seemed like a chasm.

Gray wouldn't – no, he couldn't – fail. Not after all the training. Not after Takiza had saved the lives of Rogue Shiver at the Tuna Run. He must complete this task! With one final burst, Gray closed the distance to the maredsoo. It was like swimming through syrup. He forced himself to open his jaws – despite the pressure that wanted to slam his mouth closed – and bit! His teeth sheared off the maredsoo plant at the stalk, and somehow it floated into his harness!

But then Gray saw that it wasn't luck at all. Briny had pushed the plant into position. He barely had time to chatter a final, "Th-th-thank-you!" before being pulled up and away from the pair. Gray didn't know if she had turned off her dangling light lure or if he'd shot away so fast he couldn't see it any more. From the sound of the water rushing past his ears, it could very well have been the latter. Gray's mind reeled and everything spun. He tried to make sure he wasn't actually spinning but couldn't tell. He passed an anglerfish with its light lure and thankfully left it underneath him. But Gray found *he* was upside down!

Flipping himself, he saw a distant *lightness* in the blackness. It couldn't be called light, but it was a lighter shade of the total black surrounding him. That was where home was.

Heartened, Gray willed himself to swim towards the less dark darkness. He forced his tail to stroke left and right but often got this simple order wrong, which stopped his upwards ascent and turned him sideways.

He kept his eyes fixed on the light. It was definitely light. He fouled up the order of his tail strokes yet again – left *then* right, what's so hard about that? At least there was no one around to see, he thought.

"Do you recall when I compared your swimming skill to that of a pregnant sea cow?"

Gray's heart leaped with relief and joy. He had never been so happy to see the little fish, no matter what insult was coming.

"Yes, Shiro."

"I am withdrawing my comment," the little betta said as he swam in front of Gray's left eye. "It's an insult to all pregnant sea cows. And you are late! Now follow me!" Takiza led Gray upwards. They were only a few minutes from the ledge, which was the gateway to the Maw. When Gray crested the cliff, Takiza told him, "Rest, Nulo. You've done passably well in this task."

"Thank you," Gray answered, panting.

"Thank you – what?"

"Thank you, Shiro."

Takiza nodded and moved in a blur, taking off Gray's harness and weaving a smaller harness from it. The frilly betta turned with a flourish, wearing the new harness. He looked positively heroic carrying the glowing maredsoo greenie as his fins rippled majestically in the water. "Nulo, you will swim as fast as you can to join your friends. Remember to tell them to wait for me before they do anything."

Gray was pained. There was no way he could rush the entire distance back this instant. He felt like he wanted to sleep for a week! "I can't!"

"You can't or you won't?"

"I can't! I just swam to the bottom of the ocean!" Gray protested. "Where are you going, anyway? You're rested. Can't you do it?"

"Where I am going is none of your concern," Takiza told him.

"But –"

The betta shook his fins and cut him off. "It is of no use for anyone to know what I am doing. It is useful to remind Lochlan and your friends not to attack Finnivus before I get back! Time is short, so swim!"

Gray got himself off the seabed. It felt like he weighed less than normal, but still, he was tired. So tired.

Takiza sighed irritably. "Fine!" The betta did a quick roll and a large leaf of the glowing greenie floated from the harness. "Eat!"

"I'm not hungry. I'm tired!"

"No talking! Only eating!"

Gray obeyed and closed his mouth on the still glowing greenie. He didn't feel the single leaf go into his mouth or down his throat. "Did I do it? Did I eat it?" he asked, puzzled.

All of a sudden it felt as though something had *bloomed* inside his stomach! Something hot! The feeling spread outwards in every direction, all the way to his snout and tail. It warmed Gray's body, banishing the coldness as well as his dreary thoughts. He suddenly felt he had the strength of ten sharkkind!

"YEEEE-HAAAAA!" Gray yelled as he swam in a tight circle so fast it spun the sand on the seabed into a whirling funnel.

"I will be there soon. Tell them to wait!" Takiza began moving his frilly fins in an odd pattern.

"What if that isn't possible?" Gray asked.

"Then be prepared to do the *im*possible!" Takiza said. The betta shot away so fast Gray only saw a churning wake in the water.

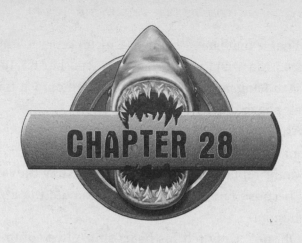

CHAPTER 28

THE MAREDSOO POWERED GRAY'S FURIOUS swim from the training grounds back home to Coral Shiver. There was a dull roar in his ears and his heart raced. But when Gray was about halfway home, the Dark Blue greenie's effects stabilized. He wasn't hungry or tired, even though he had swum at a sprinting-attack speed the whole way. Finally, he saw the Rock Lobster formation near Coral Shiver's homewaters.

A cold fear gripped Gray when he noticed a steady stream of sharkkind and dwellers leaving the hidden entrance. But then he realized it was okay. His mother and Mari were leading everyone in an organized move. Gray scanned the waters and saw nothing of Indi Shiver. Not yet, anyway. He hurried to his mum and Mari.

"What are you doing?" he asked them. "Takiza wanted you to wait."

"That would have been useful to know earlier in the day," Mari said. The thresher waved her tail for the crowd to keep moving. "Come on, come on! No time to waste!" she told everyone.

"Are you sure this is a good idea?" Gray asked his mother.

Sandy replied, "Lochlan and AuzyAuzy Shiver left early because Finnivus is going to execute the armada commander."

"Oh, no!" Gray felt his heart sink. "I've got to help! Where are they?"

Mari quickly told Gray what everyone was doing and where they were most likely to be, and he streaked off towards the Riptide homewaters. Luckily, Slaggernacks was on the way, as he wanted to make a quick stop. But no one was there. The place looked like just another series of caves and greenie-covered coral.

Gray was about to leave when he reached out with his senses and found stonefish and octos hiding among the rocks. Gray was surprised he could tell which one was Trank. He glided over to what most fins and dwellers would see as an innocent pile of rocks.

"Get up, Trank," he said. Nothing moved. For a moment he felt silly. But Gray could feel the stonefish breathing now that he was close. "Quit fooling around."

Trank didn't move, but did answer. "Wouldja keep swimmin'? Youse is attracting unwanted attention."

"You said Gafin would help, and we're going to need that help now."

"We're closed. Move along!"

Gray nudged the stonefish by swishing his large tail directly over it. "Come on!" When he tried to move the stonefish again, its spikes sprang out.

Trank turned slightly. "I told youse, we're closed."

Gray grew hot with anger. "You know what? Sharkkind say that stonefish can't be trusted. And I always stick up for you. I say, 'No, you have to get to know Trank. He's loyal.' But you're not, are you? When the current gets rough, you stick your head in the sand like a baby turtle. Well, I'm done with you. You hear that, Trank?"

But there was no answer from the stonefish. Gray shook his head, feeling more sadness than he should. The others were right: Trank wasn't to be trusted. Gray blasted away, covering the dweller with sand as he put Slaggernacks behind him.

He forced himself forward, faster and faster, trying to make up for lost time. Gray wouldn't let Lochlan and AuzyAuzy fight without him. Takiza would be angry that they hadn't waited, but it couldn't be helped. If Gray could go round to the far side of the old Goblin Shiver homewaters, he could swim into battle with the small AuzyAuzy force.

It was then that he saw a hundred Indi Shiver shark-kind rise over the crest of the Riptide homewaters.

While Gray wanted to fight, he didn't want to be

foolishly sent to the Sparkle Blue. He descended into the greenie and watched as the battle formation passed, leaving the homewaters. Gray counted and figured that it wasn't the entire armada but about a third of it.

The odds just got a little better, he thought. But this meant that two thirds of the Indi armada was still around. How could the splinter force of AuzyAuzy, along with Rogue Shiver and some sharkkind of Coral, beat Finnivus and his force of well-trained mariners? Gray had never seen the armada set a single fin out of place once they were in formation and being guided by their mariner prime.

It was then that a thought hit Gray, making him tingle all over. He hoped the tingle was because his idea was a good one, and not some funky after-effect of the maredsoo. The concept was crazy and had the longest odds of succeeding. And it would require him to wait patiently and not do anything until the *perfect* moment – something he wasn't used to doing.

But if Gray could pull it off, his friends just might have a chance against Finnivus and the Indi armada.

CHAPTER 29

"WE NEED TO MOVE SOON," ONYX WHISPERED.

They were well inside the Riptide homewaters. Barkley nodded that he understood but motioned the blacktip to stay put. He could see the royal court and Riptide's colourful terraced greenie cliffs in the background. There was nothing to do but be still. Usually Barkley could do this quite well. He prided himself on being able to outwait *and* outwit others. But this wasn't training or sneaking up to scare a friend or even hunting for lunch. So much was riding on this crazy mission that Barkley's patience was stretched to breaking point.

Ripper swam by, led by two armoured *squaline*. Barkley hissed softly, "Here we go." They were so close! But they had to wait for the signal. If they broke Whalem out of prison before it was time, every one of them would end up on Finnivus's dinner menu.

Barkley had taken a long look at Whalem's cage. It wasn't like the whale-skeleton prison he had been locked in by Velenka last year. This was different. There was no system of interlocking bars on the door. In fact, the front door looked much like the three other sides of the cage, although it did have a rectangular section with a hole in it. But there was no way a shark could get a fin into that small hole! How would they open it?

One *squaline* tugged on the chain that held Ripper. The scarred hammerhead glared, growling in a menacing tone, "Do that again and you'll be sorry."

The guard laughed. "The only thing I'll be sorry about is if I don't get a piece of you for dinner."

The other *squaline* added, "Or if you give the emperor gas!"

"Oh, that would be bad!" agreed the first one. "I'm on throne duty tonight!"

The first guard placed one of the links of the chain holding Ripper on to a pole in front of the cage housing Whalem. This had the effect of acting as a brake on Ripper while the other guard was still connected to him.

Whalem roused himself when he heard the clanking of the metal door. The first guard saw this. "Looks like you're getting company, *Commander.*" The *squaline* used the title as an insult. "Hope you two get along. Open the cage!"

For a moment, nothing happened, but then an octopus crawled out of its hiding place holding a shiny object in one of its suction-cup-covered tentacles. Barkley cursed to himself. How could he have been so stupid? He had *lived* in a landshark ship and knew landsharks had things called *keys* that opened doors and chests. So there wasn't a knob or lever to push and release Whalem. This cage could only be opened with a key!

And there was no way this Indi octo was going to give it to them! Barkley's mind raced as the octopus crawled its way up the bars, inserting the key into the lock. Had the octo heard them the last time they were here? If so, why hadn't he reported it? Did Trank have something to do with that? Trank had said Gafin had treaties with dwellers all over the Big Blue. But these were questions for another time. The door swung open! They *had* to act while it was open!

"Inside," the second guard ordered Ripper.

This was their chance! Just then there was a tremendous cry from the guards in the royal court. Barkley could hear, "Alarum! Alarum! We're being attacked!"

It was the signal!

Barkley streaked up and speared one of Ripper's guards in the liver. Onyx took care of the second. Being chained to Ripper, the smaller guard had no chance, and the hammerhead helped batter him into submission. Barkley let the octo scoot away. He was probably just another dweller forced to do the emperor's bidding.

Ripper saw and didn't approve. "You're still weak,"

he said to Barkley after spitting out the bite blocker in his mouth. "Much better," he said, gnashing his rows and rows of teeth.

Whalem crept to the edge of the cage, and Ripper moved to block the tiger. "What are you doing?" Onyx asked crossly. "We're here to get him out, not keep him in!"

"Looks like he's having second thoughts," Ripper said. "Maybe he'd like to turn us in to prove his loyalty?"

Barkley saw that Ripper was right! There *was* doubt in the armada commander's eyes. Of course, there would be. Onyx didn't want to believe it. "That's crazy! Let him out. Sir, I am so sorry."

"Lochlan says he doesn't hold you responsible," Barkley told the tiger commander. This seemed to settle the older shark, and the look of doubt went away.

Whalem nodded at Barkley. "I still have much to apologize for, though. Lead on."

The Indi armada was being arranged in its battle formation, at least ten rows deep. Barkley began picking his way through the kelp field, away from the noise and bustle.

Ripper had other ideas. He zoomed back towards the royal court!

"Where are you going?" Barkley hissed.

"To deal with Velenka!" he shouted.

Before Barkley could do anything, they were spotted. "The prisoners have escaped! The prisoners have escaped!" the *squaline* shouted.

A group of ten armoured guards streaked towards them.

"So much for the easy way!" Barkley shouted as he broke from cover with everyone else. "Swim for your lives!"

THE BATTLE OF RIPTIDE

CHAPTER 30

ONYX PASSED BARKLEY AS IF HE WERE ON A LAZY afternoon swim.

"Pick up the pace!" snapped Whalem, as he also flashed ahead.

Barkley tore after the two as fast as he could. Luckily, rather than pursuing them, the *squaline* broke away to defend Finnivus as Ripper shot towards him like a maniac.

Barkley saw Whalem head directly for the massive armada formation. "Follow me! I have an idea!" Whalem yelled. The old tiger swam directly between the growing pyramid formation of sharkkind and the new mariner prime, who was busily barking orders at everyone. Barkley's group churned past, and for a moment, the new Indi commander was too shocked to do anything. He shook his head, not believing what had just happened, then shouted, "Capture them!"

The pyramid formation seemed to melt as the sharks on the top dived into a downwards current straight at Whalem, Onyx and Barkley. The armada's subcommanders, busily carrying out their last instructions, bellowed at the Indi mariners to stay in formation. The new mariner prime then realized his mistake. "No! Wait, stop! Back to your positions!" he cried. But it was too late. The formation was hopelessly disorganized. No one could swim anywhere.

"Ha!" yelled Whalem. "That new mariner prime can't hold a lanternfish to me!"

"Go, go, go!" Barkley urged.

Onyx streaked towards the area where Lochlan and AuzyAuzy Shiver were assembling, with Barkley and Whalem close behind.

"Got him," Onyx told Lochlan as he whipped into battle position facing the Indi armada.

"Good on ya," the golden great white said, nodding. "Barkley, Snork, take the commander to the safe area. We'll hold them up long enough for you to disappear."

Whalem took only a moment to size up the hourglass formation of Lochlan's forces. The AuzyAuzy mariners were mostly on the top with the Coral Shiver sharks arranged below. This would give the more experienced AuzyAuzy mariners a chance to descend from above, using the now downward-drifting currents to their advantage. With Coral Shiver's lack of training in formation fighting, they had to be protected.

Whalem looked at Lochlan and shook his head. "You'll be slaughtered."

Barkley saw the faces of the AuzyAuzy Line and knew it was true! And yet they were still willing to swim into the battle. He couldn't believe it.

"You can't do this!" Barkley told Lochlan. "You're supposed to be the shark everyone rallies around! You can't die!"

"Very touching, mate, but you've got to leave," the golden great white replied. "Whalem will lead you. He's better than I am."

The tiger commander shook his snout vigorously. "I dishonoured myself! I will stay if your mariners will allow me to guide them."

"For the love of Tyro!" shouted Barkley. "Let's all just swim away!"

Lochlan told Whalem, "We don't have our dolphs to coordinate the formation, so we can only delay them."

The old tiger looked at Lochlan. "Have you studied the Battle of Silander's End?"

"Oh, you've got to be kidding," Kendra interrupted. "You want to use voice commands? From the centre of the formation?"

"It would have to be a two-pronged formation," Lochlan said, a toothy grin spreading across his face.

"Exactly!" agreed Whalem. "That would counter their

speed!" The two looked at each other, and Barkley could see a mutual respect grow between the old mariner and the young king.

Lochlan nodded to the old tiger. "If you wouldn't mind commanding the second battle fin, I'd appreciate it."

"I'd be honoured ... my King."

Lochlan told his Line, "Kendra, you're with me. Xander, Jaunt, you're now Whalem's subbies," meaning subcommanders.

Jaunt tail-slapped Whalem's flank. "Too right! We'll help the oldie!"

The old tiger was shocked for a moment – and then roared with laughter. Barkley supposed no one had spoken to Whalem that way for several decades.

"If today's my day to swim the Sparkle Blue, let that be the chorus of my farewell song!" Whalem called out with a smile, showing his notched teeth.

The AuzyAuzy mariners thought this was hilarious and also laughed.

Barkley turned to Snork. "Do they realize everyone might die today?"

"I think that's why they're laughing. To stop them feeling scared," the sawfish answered.

"Hey!" shouted Striiker. "Are we going to fight at some point? I thought you AuzyAuzy fins liked to fight, but all I see is a lot of yapping!"

Apparently Xander and Striiker were brothers at heart. Xander took his position ahead of the great white and yelled, "Soon enough, young son. Soon enough. That is if you don't talk them to death first and spoil the party!"

Then Whalem and Lochlan had a rapid conversation that Barkley barely understood.

"Watch their Topside Rip and Slide attacks," Whalem said. "They'll roll down the current with Orca Bears Down or Sea Snake Engarde."

"Should we be ready for Yellowfin Feeding on Minnows or Cuttlefish Strikes a Crab?" asked Lochlan. "Won't they be looking for a chance to end this early?"

"The new mariner prime won't be so bold. He outnumbers us four to one even without his third battle fin."

Barkley recognized the terms as fighting moves, but these two obviously had an entirely different level of expertise. As Lochlan and Whalem spoke, the Auzy-Auzy subcommanders moved the formation from the shape of an *X* to one made up of two *V*s, which then interlocked to form a *W*.

From his position in Lochlan's half of the formation, Barkley saw the much more massive Indi armada moving from the Riptide homewaters towards them. The armada was five levels higher than their own and in the shape of a pyramid. Barkley felt icy cold inside his stomach. How would they be able to survive Indi's attack?

"The time for chibber-chabber is done and gone!" yelled Jaunt. "Here they come!"

Both Lochlan and Whalem were well aware. "Quick

and decisive!" shouted the tiger shark commander to everyone. "That's the way to do things!"

"Agreed! Let's give 'em a good snout banging!" Lochlan exclaimed.

Lochlan and Whalem swam into the centre of their respective *V* formations. From their positions, theoretically, the subcommanders would relay their shouted orders to everyone else.

In reality, though ...

Barkley didn't understand how Lochlan and Whalem would make split-second decisions in the thick of battle while they themselves might be fighting for their lives. And even if everyone heard the commands, there was a whale-size difference between understanding an order and carrying it out!

Once it got moving, the massive Indi armada was a thing of deadly grace. Their sharks swam so close together and turned with such precision that the entire formation seemed like a single, monstrous predator. They shifted their ranks into other shapes, smoothly and cleanly. Lochlan and Whalem shouted countermoves, and their own ranks morphed and changed. But the combination of Auzy-Auzy, Rogue and Coral sharks didn't blend seamlessly like the more experienced Indi armada. Their reactions were delayed and their swimming wasn't nearly as crisp.

The Indi armada split into three battle fins of a hundred sharkkind, each one larger than the entire AuzyAuzy-Coral formation.

"Hold fast in your eights!" yelled Lochlan.

The subcommander in Barkley's section of the formation was Kendra. She translated, "Stay on my tail! Don't attack yet!"

Many sharks were out of position, and Barkley could tell some were already tired. They had had none of the training or discipline of the armada.

Then Indi's second battle wing struck! At least ten sharkkind on Barkley's side were mauled and spun crazily towards the seabed below. They followed that with feinting moves by the first and third Indi battle fins, which pulled apart the AuzyAuzy-Coral ranks as they tried to counter.

Then the second Indi battle fin attacked for real and broke through, killing another fifteen AuzyAuzy-Coral mariners. Barkley barely avoided a bite at his left fin as he struggled to keep up. He heard Lochlan yell, "Regroup! Swim through the Split S!" Kendra again translated that into something he could understand.

Barkley caught a glimpse of the flashing lanternfish device relaying signals to the Indi armada. That way of communicating was much faster. Their subcommanders didn't listen for commands but merely glanced over to *see* their orders, then acted on them. The Indi mariner prime also had the advantage of watching the entire battle waters from a safe distance. It's too much of an advantage to overcome, Barkley thought hopelessly. It's only a matter of time before they crush us.

Lochlan and Whalem *were* working miracles, though. Barkley couldn't believe how speedily their formation was reordered after their initial battering.

The first battle wing of the Indi armada did a sharp looping turn and dived from above. This time the damage was far worse. Thirty sharkkind were mortally wounded – and Indi's third battle fin, packed with heavy sharks like great whites and bulls filled the gap, preventing Lochlan and Whalem from reforming into a single defensive formation. Blood bloomed thick in the water, causing Barkley to gag.

They were about to be eaten alive!

Barkley saw the other two Indi battle fins form a pincer move. The first did another looping attack from above. It was doubtful that the AuzyAuzy-Coral force could stop *any* of the attacks, much less all of them. Barkley glanced at the lanternfish light board and knew he had made a huge mistake. He wasn't a good mariner and never would be even if he lived to be a hundred – which definitely wouldn't happen now.

"I should be sneaking up to that signaller to destroy it! I've killed us all by not using my head," Barkley muttered through gritted teeth. The Indi armada closed in for what would be a final, decisive attack.

Just when all hope seemed to be lost, Barkley caught a glimpse of an immense shark bursting from the greenie and streaking at the lanternfish signaller.

His heart leapt. It was Gray!

CHAPTER 31

GRAY BOLTED FROM THE PATCH OF THICK greenie, very close to where the Indi mariner prime hovered. It was a miracle he had made it this far. But with Whalem escaping, the royal court being attacked by Ripper and two armadas clashing a short distance away, it was the perfect storm. The utter panic and confusion inside the Riptide homewaters hid Gray better than even the thickest kelp field.

Much to Gray's surprise, for five whole seconds after he went into a roaring attack sprint, absolutely no one raised an alarm. Perhaps the few sharks who saw him streak behind the throne area where Finnivus was alternately weeping and screaming had other things on their minds.

Gray could hear the new mariner prime's orders as he closed the distance between them. "Battle fin one – Sea Serpent Strikes, execute! Battle fin two . . ." The richly tattooed armada commander, a young spinner shark, looked over an instant before Gray struck. The bite was clean and deep. Blood clouded the water as the spinner's eyes rolled upwards to the whites.

"Look out!" cried one of the subcommanders, much too late.

Gray smashed through him, and there was a free path to the signalling device. The lanternfish inside panicked, bouncing and flashing madly, but couldn't move from the enclosed mesh pen. Gray crashed into the device, breaking it to pieces in his mouth. He whipped his head from side to side, crushing the signaller further as his momentum carried him past the rim of the homewaters. Finally, Gray dropped what was left of it down a deep crevice. "Let them try and find that!"

The effect on the Indi armada was immediate. They had been doing a complex weaving manoeuvre with all three battle fins in motion at once. At least one battle fin took the panicked flashing of the terrified lanternfish as a real command from the now-dead mariner prime. That force went into an area where another was supposed to be. The two swam straight into each other!

The third battle fin tried to withdraw, but Gray's friends wouldn't let them. Lochlan bellowed, "Attack! Attack!" so loudly, it could clearly be heard across the battle waters. The AuzyAuzy-Coral formation struck the one Indi battle fin still in good order. Blood clouded everything in that area for a moment.

When the current whisked it away, Gray saw that Indi battle fin had lost over half of its sharkkind – more than fifty! The other two battle fins, in snarled confusion after swimming into each other, had no way to defend themselves when the entire AuzyAuzy and Coral Shiver force turned and charged them.

There was blood and chaos everywhere! The shrill, terrified shrieks chilled Gray's spine, but at least it wasn't his friends doing the screaming. If sharks had to swim to the Sparkle Blue today, thought Gray, let them be Indi mariners.

But the Black Wave armada wasn't going to swim away just yet. They were too disciplined. Their subcommanders saw the lanternfish weren't signalling and took matters into their own fins. AuzyAuzy tried to press its momentary advantage, but their next attack was deflected without any damage done. Then the three disorganized Indi battle fins merged into two organized ones. Even with their losses, Indi still outnumbered the AuzyAuzy force by two to one!

The armada wheeled and attacked, biting deeply into the AuzyAuzy formation. Through his lessons with Takiza and Lochlan, Gray knew they wouldn't survive another strike.

Gray sped up. He would fight to the finish with his friends. But suddenly, there was something in front of his eye – Gray thought it might be a bit of floating greenie, but then it spoke!

"Take them in, Nulo! And try not to be your usual clumsy self!"

"Takiza!" Gray shouted. "Take who in?"

"Always asking questions!" The little betta scooted upwards and behind. When Gray looked in that direction, he didn't see Takiza – but he *did* see two hundred AuzyAuzy mariners swimming towards the battle!

That was what the maredsoo greenie was for!

Takiza had swum across the entire Atlantis and into the Sific to lead the AuzyAuzy forces from there. The maredsoo had allowed them to get to Riptide in time for the battle.

The sharks of the Golden Rush, the name they used because of Lochlan's peculiar family shading, put Gray in diamond head position out in the centre and near the front. Whether he wanted to or not, Gray would lead this group into battle!

"Takiza told us to follow you," said a mako with an AuzyAuzy accent. "Orders, sir!"

Gray surveyed the situation. He was deathly afraid of doing the wrong thing but knew he needed to be decisive or his friends would die. They needed to stop the Indi armada's next attack! "We're going directly in!" he shouted to everyone around him. "Spearfisher Streaks by the Cliffs – execute!"

But his order wasn't shouted. It was relayed by the clicks and whistles of a dolphin swimming right above his dorsal fin. The AuzyAuzy mariners understood the dolphin's odd language and snapped into perfect formation.

Gray and the AuzyAuzy's forces caught the Indi armada unaware and unprotected. With a tremendous howl, the mariners of the Golden Rush ripped into their enemy. Indi had killed their king and attacked their home. AuzyAuzy showed no mercy. This attack broke the Indi armada.

Lochlan's formation merged with Gray's. "If you don't mind," the young king told him, "I'll take it from here!" Gray was happily relieved as Lochlan took the diamond head position with his personal guard and the dolphins now relayed his commands.

The subcommanders ordered everyone from Rogue and Coral to leave the formation. Now that Lochlan had his forces and the advantage of dolphins to relay his orders instantly, they would be much better without Gray and his untrained friends. The AuzyAuzy mariners smoothly and cleanly reformed and swept after the Indi armada, striking at any groups that tried to organize into a battle formation. Soon, it became a rout! The shattered Indi mariners turned tail and swam away in disarray.

In the distance, Gray saw that another large group of

sharkkind had already left. It was Finnivus and his personal guard. They were retreating. Wait! Actually, they were swimming away as fast as they could!

Gray hovered in the bloody waters in numbed shock.

Somehow, they had done it. The Battle of Riptide was won.

CHAPTER 32

AN HOUR LATER, THE LAST REMNANTS OF THE Indi Shiver armada were driven from the furthest reaches of Riptide territory. Barkley, Mari, Gray's friends from Rogue and Coral Shivers, Lochlan and all those from AuzyAuzy were talking, shouting and singing as they grieved for their lost friends.

Even Ripper was there! How did he get out of the royal court alive?

After the initial euphoria of the moment, Gray realized that the one fin he didn't see was Takiza. Where was the frilly little betta? He, most of all, deserved to be celebrating with them. Gray told everyone, "Be right back!" and quickly swam the way he'd come with the AuzyAuzy mariners. He searched and searched but found nothing. Where was Takiza?

Then Gray saw him.

But he wasn't moving.

And his gills were so still.

Gray's heart caught in his throat as he slowed himself to a hover, the little betta's body drifting with the slow current next to his left eye. For a moment the water caught Takiza's frilly fins, making them bloom splendidly, but otherwise there was no movement.

Not even a fin flick.

The eyes of Takiza Jaelynn Betta vam Delacrest Waveland ka Boom Boom stared blankly into the Big Blue.

"Takiza?" Gray said in a whisper as tears welled up in his eyes. "Takiza?"

There was no answer.

"Oh, no, no, no," was all Gray could keep repeating.

He sobbed a few times. He tried to keep his grief and pain inside, but then, like a tidal wave, everything came pouring out. How could the noble fish have sacrificed himself? For what? Finnivus was still *alive*!

Gray gave himself over to full-blown bawling for many minutes until he saw the little betta looking crossly at him, shaking his head in disapproval.

"TAKIZA!" shouted Gray.

"The first time I've slept soundly in a hundred years, and you disturb me with your hysterical sobbing!" Takiza shook himself and fluttered his gossamer fins this way and that. He grunted as if everything was to his satisfaction.

"Oh, Takiza! I –"

Gray was cut off by a sizeable tail slap across the snout that made him wince. "How many times do I have to tell you to address me as Shiro?" Takiza shook his head once more. "Of all my apprentices through the ages, Nulo, you are truly the *most* Nulo."

"But at least I'm the *best* at being worst," Gray said, grinning. "I have that going for me, right?"

The betta snorted. He caught himself and scowled. "What am I to do with you? Keep up your training, Nulo. I must see to things much more important than listening to you weep or your pathetic attempts at humour. Do try and stay out of trouble for a little while until I return!" And with that, Takiza flared his fins once more and swam away.

Gray called after him, "I'll miss you, too, Shiro!"

Takiza didn't answer as he disappeared into the Big Blue, but somehow, Gray could tell the little betta was smiling.

EPILOGUE

"I WILL KILL THEM ALL!" SHOUTED FINNIVUS. "They have dishonoured my – our! – armada! But what if they're coming after me right now? What if that evil Lochlan and his Golden Rush want to send me to the Sparkle Blue? Where are my guards? I must have more guards! I order them to protect me! And destroy the sharks responsible for this!"

Tydal watched the emperor alternate between fear and rage as what remained of their forces travelled back towards the Indi homewaters. Normally, every sharkkind in the court would fight tooth and fin to be nearest to His Highness. Not today. Most in the court stayed as far away as their rank permitted. This was a day of disaster. Tydal wouldn't be surprised if Finnivus had the whole thing wiped from the royal history. How had Whalem escaped? How had that giant hammerhead called Ripper attacked Velenka in the middle of the royal court? If it hadn't been for the quickness of the *squaline* – who had first thought Ripper was after Finnivus – she wouldn't have had a one-flippered seal's chance in a feeding frenzy of having remained with the living. As it was this aptly named Ripper had killed two of Finnivus's personal guards and *still* managed to get away!

But the most shocking thing of all was that the Indi Shiver armada had been defeated.

Tydal could only think of this in the hushed silence of his mind. The force against their mariners was smaller and not as well-trained. But they had won anyway! True, many things happened, not the least of which was a giant shark destroying the lanternfish signaller. How a fish that size managed to *sneak* into the homewaters unseen was simply baffling.

"They have not seen the last of us!" yelled Finnivus. "I am the emperor of the Big Blue, and they have rebelled against my just and gentle rule! They task me! They will pay!"

Tydal knew that once Finnivus was less panicked, he would gather his forces and bring another, far larger armada back to these waters. The tides of the entire North Atlantis would turn red with blood. How could anything stand against Finnivus's royal wrath? It was impossible.

But when Tydal had woken up this morning, he would have said any of the things that had happened today were impossible.

The armada had been defeated. Finnivus was swimming home in disgrace. There was much to think about. Tydal replayed in his mind how the emperor had shrieked when the hammerhead seemed to be hurtling towards him.

Tydal was careful not to show any emotion as he watched Finnivus sob, but inside, he laughed.

Takiza swam away with all the dignity he could muster. To be found floating in the water like a piece of drifting garbage! Absolutely galling! Little did the young pup know how close Takiza had come to swimming the Sparkle Blue. Even after giving Lochlan's mariners the maredsoo brought from the Dark Blue's depths by his increasingly capable apprentice, Takiza knew they wouldn't make it in time. He'd used his powers to speed the current, pushing it faster and faster to make up the difference.

By the time they'd arrived at the battle, Takiza could see the motes of colour dancing on the edge of his vision that preceded everyone's journey into the Sparkle Blue. He allowed himself a smile. How his apprentice had led at a moment's notice! How easily Gray had filled the role of commander! Even though Takiza had made sure to ask – a force as proud and capable as the Golden Rush would not blindly follow just anyone – they had trusted Gray with their lives upon meeting him! It gave Takiza hope for the first time in a long time.

The Indi armada had been defeated because they had been caught by surprise.

That wouldn't be the case next time.

But these were thoughts for another day.

Takiza would go to a safe place and rest. He needed to regenerate his strength, or he would surely fail. It was such a long current to swim, and he despaired of successfully completing his journey. But he would try.

Tyro would expect nothing less.

Turn the page for
a sneak peek of

Into the
Abyss

CHAPTER 1

GRAY TORE THROUGH THE WATER, MINDLESS OF the shrieking crowd all around him. His concentration was total as his huge opponent barrelled forward using an attacking move called Spearfisher Streaks by the Cliffs. Gray feinted to the left before slipping into the Swordfish Parries. There was a tremendous shock down Gray's spine as his snout struck the left flank of the ferocious great white. A solid hit!

The crowd's yells and excited thrashing vibrated the water so much that his hearing and lateral line senses were nearly useless. But the battlefield was well lit – that wasn't the problem. No, the problem was that there was absolutely no quit in his foe, who recovered quickly and zoomed straight for him once more.

I didn't even slow him down, thought Gray, gnashing his rows of curved and razor-sharp teeth in frustration.

The great white was wickedly agile, carving turns

through the water that Gray was hard pressed to deflect or defend against. But he had learned much in the months since the Battle of Riptide. "Come on, come on," Gray muttered to himself. "I know you want to do it." The huge shark tried Yellowfin Feeding on Minnows, which Gray ruined by using Waving Greenie. Then the great white went for a Topside Slide, which was a deadly dorsal fin attack. But Gray knew it was a trick. And sure enough, at the last moment the charging shark switched into his favourite move – the one Gray had been waiting for him to use – Orca Bears Down.

Gotcha! Gray thought triumphantly. He rolled into a rising current, madly churning his tail to shift sideways just enough so the hurtling shark missed him by a fin length. Then Gray streaked after the great white and performed the very same move, Orca Bears Down.

There was a satisfying "Oof!" from the great white as he was driven into the seabed. With a tail waggle he signalled surrender, and the match was over.

Gray had finally won. He had finally beaten King Lochlan Boola Naka Fiji, and it was glorious!

"Yes! Yes! I knew you would come at me with Orca Bears Down!" Gray exclaimed triumphantly as Lochlan spat sand from his mouth.

"Went to that feeding ground once too often, eh? Oh, I'm going to be tasting sand for a week! Good match, though!"

Gray flexed his pectoral fins. "I don't blame you for trying. You've beaten me, like, twenty times with it!"

The crowd watching their match, mostly sharkkind and dwellers from Rogue and Coral Shivers, began chanting, "Gray! Gray! Gray!" He waved his tail to everyone in the stadium, acknowledging the cheers. His mother Sandy was there, as were his younger brother and sister, Riprap and Ebbie. Of course his friends from Rogue were right in front. Striiker was fighting in the arena next, Gray saw. If there was fighting to be done, his first in Line would be there. But Shell, Mari, Snork and Barkley preferred to just hover and watch.

"I have to go with Lochlan," Gray told Barkley, Sandy and the others. "I'll meet you all later!"

Gray felt a small electric charge roll through the water. He looked back to the arena and sure enough, Prime Minister Shocks was motioning Striiker and an AuzyAuzy mariner forward for their match. The eel's electricity was especially useful when he wanted everyone's attention, like at dweller council meetings, where things could get a little shouty. After a few instructions to tell both combatants to keep it clean and bloodless, another bolt of electricity signalled the start of the match. Gray and Lochlan swam off, the shouts of the excited crowd rolling with them as they glided away from the training field and to their meeting with the leaders of Hammer and Vortex Shivers.

Gray sighed, finally able to relax a little. He was glad the match was over. Gray liked training, of course. But this felt more like fighting to *entertain* others. Something was just not right about that. Not when so much blood had been spilled. But taking back the Riptide homewaters from Finnivus and his armada demanded some celebration. And Lochlan told Gray that he needed to prove his worth in front of the two other shivers that were here to talk about joining their cause. Finnivus and the Indi armada had been sent swimming back to their homewaters, that was true. But the hateful emperor would be back to seek vengeance. This wasn't a matter of *if*, but *when*. That was why Lochlan had sent messengers to Hammer and Vortex Shivers.

"Besides," Lochlan told Gray, "We really should break in the place with a bang-o, doncha think?"

To Gray's thinking this whole week had been one heck of a bang-o. After long and often boisterous council meetings, Gray had decided to resurrect Riptide Shiver. After all, it had been an ancient and honourable shiver for thousands of years before Goblin, its previous leader. "And in a few years, no one will even remember that flipper," Striiker had said. Whalem's long-range scouts had confirmed that Finnivus was still in the Indi Shiver homewaters.They could breathe easy, at least for a little while, and so they had this party. Lochlan had told Gray it was a *working* party. They would work to gain allies during the festivities. Almost everyone else treated it like a party-party, though.

I wish I could, thought Gray.

Even though there was laughter and excitement

because of today's celebration, underneath that he felt a dreadful tingle in the water. It was the feeling of danger, not close right now, but coming for sure. Gray thought back to the momentous event that was the reason for the celebration. *And* the reason every fin should be on edge.

It had been six months since the combined forces of AuzyAuzy, Coral and Rogue Shivers had defeated the Indi armada and sent Emperor Finnivus frantically swimming all the way back to the Indi Ocean and his own homewaters. Finnivus was a cruel and vicious tiger shark, the leader of an ancient shiver that wanted to conquer all the Big Blue. The emperor had been miraculously beaten, but Finnivus wasn't the type of fin to forgive and forget. He would return to wipe them out. And that was why, even though the celebration was fun, Gray couldn't shake the feeling in the water that seemed to say, "Watch your tails, everyone. Watch your tails."

TO BE CONTINUED . . .

ACKNOWLEDGEMENTS

Thanks to all the great people at Razorbill for putting up with me, but most of all Ben Schrank, who took a huge chance by choosing someone who never wrote a book before; Jessica Rothenberg, past super-editor, future super-novelist; Emily Romero, Erin Dempsey, Mia Garcia, Shanta Newlin, Bernadette Cruz and everyone else from marketing and pubicity; also Gillian Levinson and finally Laura Arnold, my fin-tastic Shark Wars editor.

Special thanks to everyone in Los Angeles who helped me over the years but especially the awesome Jim Krieg, who I met in film school and who despite that still picks up the phone when I call; John Semper, who hired me first; Mark Hoffmeier, great writer and fantasy football superstar. Also my friends from Notre Dame, Go Irish! And finally my sister Jude, who's not the most annoying sister in the world, most of the time.

Visit **www.SharkWarsSeries.com** to learn more
and to play the Shark Wars game!

ERNEST JOHN ALTBACKER is a screenwriter who has worked on television shows including *Green Lantern: The Animated Series*, *Ben 10*, *Mucha Lucha* and *Spider-Man*. He lives in Hermosa Beach, California. *Shark Wars* is his first book.